ONLY JANE

Only Jane

by *Molly Cone*

DRAWINGS BY VELMA ILSLEY

THOMAS NELSON & SONS

Edinburgh   NEW YORK   Toronto

Library of Congress Catalog Card Number: 60-7288

To Jerry

ONLY JANE

CHAPTER ONE

"You think it's really a horse?" Merilee asked absently, giving most of her attention to her Coke.

Jane tried to snort. "Well, hardly," she said, but her heart began to beat more rapidly.

There was no particular reason why Jane should expect her birthday surprise to be a horse. Certainly neither her mother nor her father had indicated any intention of buying a horse for her. They hadn't asked her what she wanted for her fifteenth birthday. But she had hinted, Jane reflected as she pushed the straw into the tall glass of Coke; she'd surely hinted often enough.

Jane Taylor and Merilee Kennedy were sitting at the soda counter of Schaffer's Drug Store. In the mirror behind the soda fountain they could see the prescription counter, the cosmetic case, and the magazine stand. Through the window they could see the sidewalk. It was the best place to sit, according to Merilee, far better than a booth. What she meant, Jane knew, was that it was the best place to watch the boys go by.

Jane felt Merilee's gaze on her. She pretended not to notice, but she knew it was one of admiration. Merilee was afraid of horses. She was even reluctant to pet the ponies at the Woodland Park Zoo.

But Merilee's expression changed quickly as Woody Neilson, who lived in the house behind Jane's and never so much as looked at her, passed the store.

"Hi, Merilee!" he shouted through the open door.

"Oh, hi!" Merilee called; then she bent to touch her lips to the straw. She seemed intent on her drink.

Her lashes, Jane noticed, made long shadows on her cheeks. She wore bright pink lipstick, and her figure—Involuntarily Jane sighed.

Jane's legs and arms were long. She was, she sometimes thought, all legs, like the colt at the riding stable. Merilee, on the other hand, seemed to be cut all from one piece. She was small and compact, she had curves instead of angles, and she curled her eyelashes; once she had even "rinsed" her hair. Jane knew, because Merilee had confided this to her. Jane had nothing to confide in return—except her desire for a horse.

She tried to recapture Merilee's attention. "It's funny how they always seem to know just what I want the most," said Jane with a sudden surge of love for her parents.

Merilee raised her head and looked through the window. She said, "Imagine! A horse! Do you think that's what the surprise will really be?"

8

Though she had already asked the question, Jane considered it carefully. By concentrating, she could almost erase from her mind the picture of Woody Neilson waving through the door—to Merilee. Woody was a junior. He was on the track team and he was a regular on the high school football team.

Jane brought her thoughts firmly back to the horse. She could use the garage for a stable. Lots of people left their cars in the street all the time; there was no reason why her father couldn't leave his there. Her thoughts hurried on. The horse would be a thoroughbred, a little mare. It would be delivered in a horse trailer, and it would put its head on Jane's shoulder and whinny. Bonny, her favorite horse at the riding stable, rarely did this; usually she only blinked as Jane mounted her. A horse of her own! The idea filled her mind completely—almost.

Merilee nudged her. "Look who's at the prescription counter," she whispered.

As Jane looked into the mirror, the girl standing at the counter across the store raised her eyes and smiled at Jane's reflection. "Hi!" she said to the mirror.

Jane smiled. "Hi, Judy!" she called. Then she turned self-consciously to her drink.

"Judy Anderson," said Merilee; there was no expression in her voice.

"I think she's nice," said Jane, pleased that Judy had noticed her. She wished she knew Judy better.

"Nice." Merilee's tone was saccharine. Jane looked at her questioningly. "Well, nice if that's what you like."

Merilee dabbed at the ice in the bottom of her glass with the straw. "Personally, I think she's too—too nice, if you know what I mean."

Jane took another sip of her drink. She wasn't sure she did know what Merilee meant. But she nodded, pretending to.

"What do you think of Charlotte?" she asked casually. Charlotte was Judy's best friend. Before Jane began to go around with Merilee, she had envied Charlotte.

"Fat!" said Merilee, dismissing her with one word.

"Carol?" Carol had been the secretary of their class last year.

"Stuck up," stated Merilee.

They were quiet as they watched Judy pay the clerk and leave the store. Then Jane said, "Good heavens, Merilee! Those girls belonged to the very best crowd in junior high."

"Crowd-shmowd," replied Merilee, shrugging her shoulders and rolling her eyes.

Jane had to laugh. Merilee was such a clown. And she really didn't mean half of what she said.

"I don't believe in crowds," said Merilee, noisily sipping the last of her Coke through the straw. "Stay away from any crowd—that's my motto."

Jane finished her drink, and nodded. She'd never felt comfortable in a crowd herself. She and Merilee were very much alike. Happily she wiped her lips on the paper napkin. Reaching into her pocket, she counted out five pennies and a nickel. All of her allowance went for riding, but she had to do baby-sitting to make enough to ride even once a week. Jane put the money on the counter and slid off the stool.

Merilee was searching her pockets. "Oh, darn!" she said, "I forgot. I only have a nickel."

The boy behind the counter picked up the coins, tossed a nickel into the air and caught it. He pegged the cash register.

Merilee smiled at him. "You don't really want a whole dime for that tiny little Coke, do you?"

The boy looked at her. "That's the price, miss," he said.

Merilee pouted. "But—"

Jane felt a blush mounting from her neck to her forehead. Quickly she put her hand in her pocket. "Come on, Merilee," she whispered. "I'll lend you a nickel." She put the nickel on the counter.

Merilee laughed at the boy over her shoulder. He grinned at her. "I'll pay you back tomorrow," she said to Jane.

The girls strolled up the street together.

"Do you think he's going to ask you to the club dance?" Jane suddenly felt impelled to ask.

"Who? Woody? Who cares?" Merilee answered lightly. But a pleased smile was already curling the corners of her mouth. "Anyway," she said, with a grimace, "my mom said I can't have *another* formal this summer—even if he does ask me."

Jane looked at her a moment. *She* didn't even own one formal, and Merilee might soon have two.

The club dance was always formal, Jane knew. There was sort of an unwritten law that you had to be in the first year of senior high before you could attend the club dance, although Merilee had gone last year and no one had noticed the difference. Of course, she had only gone with her cousin, but still she had gone. And it had been a beautiful dance last year. Jane knew that, because Merilee had told her all about it. There had been frosted stars hanging from the ballroom ceiling, punch was served in the lounge, and there had been real "live" music—an orchestra. The club dance was *the* event of the summer for the younger crowd, and it was held just before Labor Day. You just weren't *anybody* if you didn't go.

She couldn't imagine anyone's asking *her* to the dance even though it was two whole months away. She reflected now that she had hardly spoken to a boy in her life—outside of school; she didn't even know how to. Things like that came easily to Merilee. But then Merilee had a raft of brothers, and Jane—well, Jane had never even had a kitten, or puppy, to say nothing of a horse. Her mother was allergic to cats and dogs. Oh, how she hoped the birthday surprise would be a horse! A horse of her own. As long as she could remember she had wanted a horse more than anything in the world.

Merilee stopped suddenly. She nudged Jane. Coming toward them were Woody Neilson and two other boys.

Jane didn't stop to think. Hastily she turned away. "Good-by," she said to Merilee, "I have to go now." But before she had time to take a step, Merilee clutched her wrist.

"Stand still!" she commanded, without moving her

lips. "Hi there!" she called, waving to Woody. Jane stood still.

Woody slowed his steps. The two boys with him were Barry Mitchell and Hank Cooke. Jane knew their names, for they had been in her Spanish class last year. Politely, she nodded to them. They nodded curtly.

"We were just talking about the club dance," said Merilee.

Jane blushed. She kept her head down.

"Oh, that rat race!" said Hank.

"Who wants to go to an old club dance?" asked Barry.

Woody said nothing, but he seemed to look at Merilee with more interest. There was a long silence.

"Guess what?" Merilee spoke fast and gaily. "There's a big surprise waiting for Jane at home and she suspects— Well, she's almost certain that it's a *horse*."

The boys' heads turned toward Jane. Barry emitted a long, low whistle. Hank said, "Wow!" And Woody looked at her as though he were seeing her for the first time. Her heart gave a queer little leap.

"How lucky can you be?" Woody said.

"Well," said Jane, "it's supposed to be a surprise, you know. That is, I'm not really sure—"

Merilee said, with confident emphasis, "Well, you'll just have to *act* surprised, Jane. My goodness, think of all the trouble your parents have gone to. Why, you owe it to them to act as if the thought of a horse of your own had never entered your mind. If it was me, I'd just swoon with delight." She rolled her eyes and flung her head back, pretending she was about to faint.

13

Jane wished that Merilee wouldn't be so—well, so conspicuous. "I guess I'd better go now," she said quickly. The eyes of the three boys were on her and she felt her face redden. Merilee saved her.

"Oh, yes," Merilee said, "we must be going."

"Hey, what's the hurry?" Woody asked.

"Yeah, what's the hurry?" the other boys echoed.

Merilee turned her most brilliant smile on all three of them. Jane noted its effect with interest. "Wouldn't you like to know?" Merilee said and, grabbing Jane's arm, she walked quickly in the other direction. Jane walked very straight, conscious of the three pairs of eyes on their backs. The girls' gait, with their arms locked tightly, was rather lopsided for Jane was half a head taller than Merilee and she walked stiffly, while her friend almost danced along the sidewalk.

They heard the whistle, clear and sharp, behind them. Merilee giggled. The whistle, of course, was for her. When they had turned the corner, Jane drew a deep breath. It was surprisingly easy to talk to boys. It had never occurred to her how easy it was. She clung to Merilee's arm.

"Did you notice how they *looked* at you?" she demanded.

Merilee answered quickly, "And how they looked at you?"

For no reason at all, laughter overwhelmed them. Jane felt silly and, with Merilee beside her, she felt brave. The girls giggled intermittently as they walked toward the shopping center. When they met people, they put their heads

The boys' heads turned toward Jane.

close together, as if they were sharing a delightful secret. It seemed to Jane that no one was brighter or prettier than Merilee. She was proud when people turned to look at them. An old gentleman smiled at them and said, "That's right, girls. You're only young once!"

Jane and Merilee laughed as if he had said something terribly witty.

Yes, Jane felt silly—and gay and self-confident. It was a good feeling. It seemed to Jane that she had felt neither gay nor self-confident since the summer had begun.

In September she would be a sophomore in high school. Jane had honestly tried to take stock of herself, of her assets and liabilities; to consider how she could make the most of herself in the important years ahead. In spite of her high scholastic average, it seemed that her liabilities far outnumbered her assets. She sighed. She was smart enough in school. Why, then, did she feel so stupid outside of school?

Once she had asked her best friend to name her greatest liability: Merilee had considered the question carefully. Finally, she had said, "Well, I guess it's just that you're too serious."

Although Jane hated this description of herself, she had to agree with it. She had always been considered a "serious" child. Her mother was always saying, "Well, Jane, there's no need to take this so seriously!"

Perhaps that was why she had been so pleased when Merilee became her friend. No one could, by any stretch of imagination, call Merilee "serious." She was smart enough to make fairly good grades without half-studying, but she really didn't care. She was lighthearted and gay; she was always fun to be with. She's good for me, thought Jane, although she was well aware that her mother didn't think so.

"Not that I believe in choosing your friends for you," her mother had said when Merilee and Jane had begun to live in each other's pockets, as Mr. Taylor deprecatingly put it.

Jane, feeling loyal and adult, had refused to listen to any of her parents' criticisms of her best friend. She would have liked to tell her mother how lucky she was that Merilee had chosen to be her friend, but she thought that it would be childish to do so.

Now she tucked her arm happily through Merilee's and they walked up the street. They passed the bakery and paused before the window of a shoe store. Jane thought she had never seen such beautiful shoes. One pair especially caught her eyes; she pulled her arm from Merilee's and stood with her fingers on the plate glass. It was a pair of startlingly lovely pink slippers—the kind you'd wear with a formal—with high heels. They were marked $12.95. Jane had never worn high heels. She took a long, deep breath.

Suddenly Merilee grasped her arm. "Come on!" she cried.

Jane followed her into the store. Merilee halted as a salesman came toward them. She nudged Jane, then she turned to the salesman and said in a loud, clear voice, "We'd like to see a pair of riding shoes for my friend."

Jane gasped. She had never owned riding shoes. She had always worn her old saddle shoes when she rode.

"My friend is getting a horse," said Merilee, "and—"

The salesman nodded politely. He seemed to be really interested in Jane's getting a horse. He was sorry, he said, that the store didn't carry riding shoes in stock, although they were available on order. He asked Jane what size she wore and if she'd mind waiting ten days for the order to be filled.

"Ten days!" exclaimed Merilee. "That's an awfully long time to wait."

Jane spoke up hastily. "Perhaps I'd better think about it a while," she said to the salesman. "I'm not sure—"

"Of course," he said. "You think about it." He smiled at her. "My, aren't you the lucky one! Whenever you're ready, come in."

"Oh, we will," said Merilee. "We certainly will!"

"Thank you," said Jane as politely as she could.

When they were on the sidewalk again, they looked at each other in awe.

"Of course, you'll have to have real riding shoes," said Merilee.

"Of course," Jane agreed.

They walked on, but Jane's lighthearted mood had vanished. She looked straight ahead and no longer clung to Merilee's arm. Suddenly she remembered the book.

"Oh," she said, "my library book!"

"What library book?" said Merilee. She had pulled out her lipstick and was busily applying it to her lips.

"Remember that library book of mine you borrowed? It's due tomorrow."

"Don't worry about it," said Merilee. "It's only a library book."

Jane tried not to frown. "I'm not *worrying*," she said. "It's just that it's due tomorrow."

Merilee put the lipstick in her purse. "I'll return it. I have to go to the library tomorrow anyway."

She hummed as they went along. At the corner they met Mrs. Taylor's friend, Mrs. Almvig.

"Why, Jane," said Mrs. Almvig, "you are just the girl I want to see!" She paused, shifting a fat baby from one arm to the other, and smiled at Jane.

"Hello, Mrs. Almvig," said Jane. She reached out to tickle Johnny's fat knee.

"Will you sit with Johnny two weeks from Saturday night?" asked Mrs. Almvig.

"Sure," said Jane.

Mrs. Almvig heaved a sigh of relief. "Oh, Jane, I knew I could depend on you," she said. "I'll call you about the time later."

"Hello, Mrs. Almvig," said Merilee sweetly.

Mrs. Almvig looked at Merilee sharply. It seemed to Jane that women like Mrs. Almvig and her mother always looked at Merilee sharply. Just because she's pretty, thought Jane, and because boys like her. Well, Merilee was her best friend and Jane didn't care what Mrs. Almvig thought. Loyally she put her arm through Merilee's as they watched Mrs. Almvig hurry across the street and disappear in the supermarket.

Merilee squeezed her arm. "You know, I really think he's going to ask me to that dance."

Jane scarcely heard her. She was thinking of something else. "What if it isn't a horse?" she said.

Jane left Merilee in front of her house and, crossing the street, turned toward her own. She tried not to think of anything. But she couldn't stop thinking of the horse. She was to receive her birthday present from her parents when her father came home from his office.

"Well," the postman had said to her this morning when he had handed her a birthday post card from her Aunt Harriet. "Are you really fifteen?" He had shaken his head at the wonder of it.

Now that she thought of it, Jane recalled that people were always shaking their heads in wonder at her chronological age, even though she was so tall.

"Jane is young for her age," her mother was always saying significantly, and it made Jane uncomfortable to hear her. What her mother meant, she knew, was that she didn't have dates. Other girls of her age had dates with boys all the time. Yet Mrs. Taylor always made the remark as if it were something to be proud of. But her mother hoped she would be invited to the club dance. Jane didn't know how she knew this, but she did. Suddenly she realized how disappointed her mother would be if she *didn't* have a date for the club dance. Jane walked faster.

But perhaps she would be invited. What if the phone were to ring this evening? What if it would be Woody Neilson calling? Of course, he wouldn't ask her to the dance right away. First, he would inquire casually about her horse.

Jane stood still. She clenched her hands. And then she ran. "Oh, please let it be a horse," she whispered. "Please, please, don't let it be anything but a horse!"

CHAPTER TWO

No horse trailer stood before the Taylors' house or in the driveway beside it. There was nothing that resembled a trailer or a horse anywhere on the block. Jane rushed through the front door and looked hastily around the hall, though she hardly expected to see a horse in the house.

"Jane?" Her mother's voice came from the kitchen. Jane nodded, not trusting herself to speak.

"Is that you, Jane?" her father called. He came toward her from his den, a pleased, expectant expression on his face, a conspiratorial smile on his mouth.

Her mother hurried out of the kitchen. "Happy birthday, Jane," Mrs. Taylor said; putting her hands on her daughter's shoulders, she kissed her.

"Now close your eyes," her father ordered.

Jane gulped. She closed her eyes. Maybe, she thought wildly, they've hidden the horse in the kitchen! But she wasn't being led toward the kitchen. She was being drawn into her father's den. The room smelled of books and Dad's pipes.

"Happy birthday, Jane." It was a strange, tiny voice. It was hardly a voice at all.

Jane opened her eyes wide. On her father's desk was a cage, and in the cage was a small blue bird. It opened its mouth.

"Happy birthday, Jane," the bird said.

She felt the lump begin to rise in her throat. How could she tell them that she wanted a horse? How could she tell them she'd told everybody that she was going to get a horse? She'd told Merilee and the salesman in the shoe store and Woody and the other boys!

"Happy birthday, Jane. Happy happy birthday," the bird said.

Jane put her hands to her eyes and burst into tears. Through her fingers she could see the look of astonishment on her father's face as he stood open-mouthed with his pipe halfway to his lips. She could see the expression of dismay on her mother's face.

"But Jane dear," said Mrs. Taylor, "we thought you *wanted* a parakeet."

"But I never said I did!" she cried.

Her mother looked at her reprovingly. "We won't discuss whether you did or didn't say so. But you have received a gift. Your father and I are sorry that it isn't what you wanted—whatever that was—but I can't allow you to be so rude, to forget that it isn't the gift but the love behind the gift that counts. Jane," she said, and there was sorrow in her voice, "I am thoroughly, I am utterly disappointed in you."

Jane herself was thoroughly and utterly disappointed.

She turned abruptly and, with one arm over her face, ran to her room.

"Jane, Jane!" Her father's voice thundered up the stairs after her.

Quickly she closed her bedroom door. Only a mumble reached her now, a hum of voices that went up and down, up and down. She threw herself on the bed and pressed her face into the pillow.

Jane tried to hate her father, but she found it impossible to do that. He was the one, she felt, who understood her. He was the one who never scolded her or reminded her to pick up her room or to clear the table; who never suggested that she should wash her own stockings. What hurt most, she told herself, was that Dad, of all people, hadn't realized what she wanted most in the world—a horse.

The parakeet, she was sure, had been her mother's idea. Then she remembered how she had wept—oh, so long ago —because her mother hadn't allowed her to bring a parakeet home from the county fair. She turned over and looked at the ceiling. Her mother must have thought it was something Jane still wanted. But she had wanted a parakeet last fall, she reflected, and she had been only a child then.

Jane lay on the bed until the hum of voices from downstairs had ceased. She turned her eyes to the picture of a horse on the wall. It reminded her of Bonny, her favorite, and tears again came to her eyes. Jane liked to believe that Bonny recognized her whenever she went to the stable. When she took the river trail, she always pretended that she and Bonny were alone in a wilderness of spreading firs and elms and willows. She pretended that they would ride on and on until night came, when she would curl up on a bed of pine needles and the faithful Bonny would stand guard over her.

Downstairs the kitchen screen door slammed; the lid of the garbage can rattled. The door slammed again. Jane sat up on her bed. She wiped her eyes with her knuckles. Then she got up, opened her door, and listened. Her father was using the telephone in the kitchen. She listened until she heard him hang up. She made sure that he was not coming upstairs before she went down the hall to the little table that held the extension telephone. Reluctantly she put her hand on the telephone. She guessed she'd better tell Merilee. Jane dialed the number; Merilee answered.

"I didn't get it," said Jane, speaking softly into the telephone.

"Get what?" asked Merilee.

"The horse." Jane's voice broke.

"Oh, that!" said Merilee. "You didn't really think you would get it, did you?"

Jane stared at the telephone, amazed. "But I thought you—that is, you told them—"

Merilee's laugh came lightly over the telephone; it was almost mocking. "Well, honestly! I had to say something that would make them sit up and take notice, didn't I?"

Jane gulped.

"Oh, my goodness, Jane!" said Merilee. "Don't take everything so *seriously!*" She hung up.

Jane placed the phone on its cradle. She wondered, for

the first time since she had known Merilee, whether it had been altogether wise to discuss her greatest fault with another. She remembered the day she had met Merilee. Jane had been feeling lost and alone in the crowded corridor. It was her first day in junior high. All the children she had gone through grade school with seemed to have disappeared into classrooms that were not hers. She hesitated at the door to each room, looking at the number. The corridor was emptying rapidly. Jane cringed at the thought that she might not find the room until after the bell had rung; then she would have to walk in, before all those strange faces. Suddenly she had seen a girl hurrying toward her.

"You aren't, by any chance, looking for Room 207, are you?" the girl had asked.

Jane nodded. "I thought they'd made a mistake on my card," she admitted shyly. "I was sure there was no such room. I've looked and looked."

Merilee took her arm as if they were old friends. "I can't find it either," she giggled. It didn't seem to bother her at all. They came to a door marked 207½.

"Wait a minute," said Merilee. She opened the door and stuck her head into the room. "Is this 207?" Jane heard her ask in a pert voice.

A chorus of masculine voices shouted, "No!" Merilee closed the door.

"Well, anyway, we know that's not 207," she said, grinning. "It looked like the machine shop."

Jane gasped in admiration. She wouldn't have dared poke her head in that room, not in a thousand years!

"It's the sewing class we want," she said looking at her card again. "Maybe that's it, right next door."

The girls went into the sewing room together, and they didn't stop giggling until the teacher rapped for order. They sat next to each other, and later they met and walked home together. They had been best friends ever since then. Oh, Merilee was brash all right. But it was her brashness that had attracted Jane to her in the first place.

Jane went into the bathroom and washed her face. She stared at herself in the mirror long and thoughtfully. How she wished she had long sleek hair that turned under at the ends, like Merilee's! Jane's hair was curly, almost too curly, and there was too much of it, she decided.

She rummaged in a dressing-table drawer for her mother's nail scissors. Then she pulled a strand of hair forward so that she could see it. Using one blade of the scissors as a razor, she ran it across her hair. Jane studied the effect in the mirror. Picking up another strand, she repeated the process. Quickly she parted her hair in the center, took a deep breath, and cut bangs across her forehead.

Again she looked into the mirror. The bangs made her eyes look much larger, she decided. She studied the effect from the side with the aid of a hand mirror.

There was a light knock at the door. Hastily Jane tried to scoop up the bits of hair that had fallen into the washbowl.

"Come in," she called. She turned to face her mother, raising her eyebrows, waiting for a comment.

"Why, Jane," said Mrs. Taylor. "That looks nice! It's very becoming."

There was a note of relief in her mother's voice, as though she had been standing on tiptoe and had now sunk back on her heels. "Go down and surprise your father," she said. "Let's hear what he says."

Jane followed her mother out of the bathroom and down the hall. She could hear the parakeet chattering, "Happy birthday, Jane. Happy, happy."

Jane laughed. "Oh, that crazy bird!" she exclaimed. "Wherever did you get such a crazy bird?"

Her mother laughed, too. "Your father chose it for you," she said fondly. "He's had it in his office for a week and has spent hours teaching it to say your name."

Jane paused at the top of the stairs. She swallowed hard. She put her hand up and brushed something from her eyelids. She wished she knew what to 'say to her mother; but she didn't.

Her mother said it for her. "I can't blame you for being a bit *surprised*," she said. "It simply floored me, too."

Her mother went on talking. She sounded pleased. "Oh, by the way, that nice little Judy Anderson called and asked you to a party two weeks from Saturday night. I said you would call her."

Jane's voice faltered. "A party?"

Her mother turned to her quickly. "Why, yes. Two weeks from this Saturday night, is what she said."

"Oh, Mother!" Jane said, and it seemed to her that nothing would ever go right for her again, "I promised Mrs. Almvig I'd baby-sit that Saturday night!"

"Oh?" Her mother was walking down the stairs. A little wrinkle appeared between her eyebrows. She seemed to have forgotten about getting Mr. Taylor's reaction to the new hair-do, for as soon as she reached the lower hall, she turned with a purposeful air.

"Jane, I see no reason," she said, "why you couldn't get someone to take your place. I'm sure Mrs. Almvig wouldn't mind, under the circumstances."

"You mean it would be perfectly all right if I get somebody else?" Jane asked.

"Perfectly all right, I'm sure," said her mother confidently.

Jane flew to the telephone. But her father was there before her. He was leaning against the kitchen desk, the telephone held close to his ear, an expression of intense concentration on his face.

"Well, try them again," he said into the telephone. "And keep trying," he added, a shade louder.

Jane stood on one foot and then on the other. Her father waved her away. "Yes," he said. "Yes, I'll be here. I'll keep the line open." He hung up.

"Oh, Daddy!" Jane cried.

"It's that Olson deal," Mr. Taylor said to his wife. "There's been a mix up on the delivery, and Olson is coming up in a couple of weeks with the new contract. I told him we'd take him out to dinner. Now I'm waiting for the report on the equipment."

Jane couldn't make heads or tails of this information but her mother nodded understandingly. "I'll wear my new black," she said, as if that had anything to do with anything.

Then she turned to Jane. "I'm sure you'll have plenty of time to find a substitute tomorrow. After all, you have two weeks, you know."

She stood with her index finger on her chin looking at Jane. Jane felt herself twitching. She raised her hand to touch her bangs.

"Very nice!" her father nodded.

Jane smiled. "Well, I've never worn my hair like this before."

"Well," said her father, "you've never been fifteen before."

"That's right." Jane paused before saying, "I—I've never had a talking bird before either."

Her father smiled at her. "Well, come to think of it, you haven't, have you?"

Suddenly she could return his smile. "Thank you, Daddy. I forgot to thank you."

Her mother seemed to have come to a decision. "Jane," she said, "tomorrow we'll go down to Davis's and look for a dress for you. My goodness! This will be your first evening dress!"

Jane looked at her mother in wonder. "You mean a formal?"

Her mother nodded. "I mean a formal!" she said.

CHAPTER THREE

The next afternoon Jane stood facing the mirror in a dressing room of Davis's Fashion Shop. Reluctantly she raised her arms and let her mother and the saleswoman pull over her head a frothy dress with a ruffled skirt.

"It's her *first* formal," Mrs. Taylor confided to the saleswoman.

Jane frowned at her mother. She looked at herself in the mirror. All she could see was ruffles.

"Sweet," said the saleswoman.

"Quite nice," said Mrs. Taylor.

"I don't especially like it," Jane said in a small voice.

Her mother sighed.

The saleswoman's voice held practiced cheerfulness. "Now, why don't we let Mother go out and run through the racks again?"

Mrs. Taylor pulled back the curtain of the dressing booth and went out. Before lifting her arms to take off the dress, Jane closed the curtain tightly again. It embarrassed her to stand there in her bra and panties while people were walking past the door.

The saleswoman threw the dress over her arm. "It was really very sweet on you, my dear," she said.

Jane made a face. Then, realizing how rude that was, she explained quickly, "It makes me look too fat."

The saleswoman said in a shocked tone, "Fat? Oh, my dear! If I had a figure like yours!"

She went out, pausing to close the curtains behind her. As soon as she had gone, Jane turned to the full-length mirror. It had never occurred to her that she had a "figure." She looked at herself with interest. The curtain blew back, and hastily she grabbed her sweater and held it in front of her. Her mother came in; a little wrinkle creased her forehead. Over her arm was a dress, crisp and white. She held it up. The skirt swirled enchantingly, the neck was round and high, the bodice was sleeveless, and at the waist was one carefully placed, perfect pink rose. It was a beautiful dress.

"Oh, Mother!" Jane breathed.

"You may as well try it on," said her mother, looking at the price tag as if she had some reservations.

Jane held her arms up. The dress slipped over her shoulders. It fit snugly around her waist, and swirled about her hips with deft flattery. Jane looked at herself in the mirror. She couldn't believe her eyes. She looked slim and tall and *pretty*. "Oh, Mother!" was all she could say.

The saleswoman came in, and paused. "Yes," she said, "that's just the one I was looking for!"

Mrs. Taylor frowned. "Well, it's a little *more* than I expected to pay—"

Jane whirled to face her. "Oh, Mother!" she said for the third time, and she couldn't hide the anguish within her.

The saleswoman stood with her head on one side, looking at Jane. "Beautiful!" she said. "It might have been made for her."

Jane's mother pursed her lips and twitched at the skirt. "Are you sure it isn't too tight, dear?" she asked.

"Oh, no!" cried Jane. Her waist, she could see, looked just about as big as *that*.

"Well—" her mother began.

"You've made a wise choice," said the saleswoman. "All those other dresses were just dresses. This"—and she twitched at the skirt, too—"well, this is really something."

Mrs. Taylor laughed. "I can't wait to hear what your father says."

Jane breathed a sigh of relief. Dreamily she looked at herself in the mirror. "I saw a pair of slippers that would be absolutely perfect with this," she said. "Tiny high heels. And the same pink as the rose." She touched the flower at her waist.

"Now, Jane," her mother said firmly, "this is quite enough. Anyway, I'm sure your white flats will do very nicely."

Jane tried to hide her disappointment, as she began to do mental arithmetic. If she didn't ride for a while and if she did some extra baby-sitting, she could save enough money to buy the pink slippers. But could she save enough before Judy's party? Then she remembered that she hadn't

33

yet found a substitute baby-sitter for that Saturday night. She would have to start phoning as soon as she got home.

She added the figures again and again in her mind, as she followed her mother docilely from the dress shop to the variety store, to the budget basement of a department store. She held the dress box tightly to her.

Jane had her riding money for next week; that was three dollars. She needed nine dollars and ninety-five cents. Most girls got fifty cents an hour for baby-sitting, but she had always charged only thirty-five cents. Jane decided that she would charge fifty cents, too. Except to Mrs. Almvig. She couldn't bring herself to charge Mrs. Almvig more than thirty-five cents an hour.

She frowned as she multiplied and divided. She must remember to count the five cents that Merilee owed her. Jane pursed her lips thoughtfully, and started again. The shoes were twelve ninety-five. She needed nine ninety-five. How many hours of baby-sitting would she have to do?

She followed her mother to the glove counter and sat beside her, holding the figures in her head. Only two weeks to do all that baby-sitting! Of course, there was her allowance. She shook her head. No, she had already counted that as her riding money.

She tried to think of the different places she might work as a baby-sitter. The Almvigs' house was one, and Jane would call as soon as she got home. Perhaps Mrs. Almvig would have some daytime baby-sitting for her. Jane shook her head again. Mrs. Almvig didn't go out in the daytime often.

Jane tried to remember the names of all the families in the neighborhood with young children. There was Mrs. Everett, and that woman with the twins. And Mrs. Hokinson had a grandchild. She crossed that name off; Mrs. Hokinson's grandchild had been sent back to his parents.

She wondered if she should put an ad in the newspaper. "Baby-sitting," she might say. "Reliable girl will care for —maybe 'amuse' would be better—your children, fifty cents an hour."

She decided against *amuse*. People might think that she did magic tricks or something. Then it occurred to her that the advertisement would cost something. She didn't know how much.

"How much does an advertisement in the classified section cost?" she asked a salesgirl who was sorting gloves into drawers.

The girl looked at her blankly. "I think you have the wrong department," she said.

"Aren't these beautiful?" asked Mrs. Taylor.

Jane looked at the gloves on her mother's hands. White. They looked like any white gloves.

"I guess so," she said, still wondering who would know how much the advertisement would cost.

She heard her mother sigh. "Well, come along," she said.

Jane stood up, the dress box still clasped close to her chest.

"My goodness!" her mother exclaimed, looking at her

watch. "Where has the day gone? Do you know it's five o'clock?"

"Five o'clock!" Jane echoed. And she had all those calls to make!

Her mother began to walk briskly toward the Fifth Street entrance. Jane, who had turned the other way, swung around and loped after her.

"Well, aren't we going home?" she asked breathlessly.

"We're going out to dinner!" her mother announced.

Jane groaned.

Her mother looked at her sharply. "My goodness, Jane," she said, "I don't understand you lately. Aren't you at all pleased?"

She didn't wait for an answer. "It seems to me that with all this fuss being made over you, you could act a little more appreciative. After all, it isn't every night that we go out for dinner!"

Jane looked around. Her mother's voice had been rising higher and higher.

"Sure, I'm pleased," she said quickly. She ducked her head and fell a step or two behind her mother. She hoped people would think she was alone. But her mother slowed her pace.

"Where are we going for dinner?" said Jane, pretending to be pleased.

"Is there any special place you'd like to go?" Mrs. Taylor asked.

Jane shrugged. Then fearing that her mother might think this showed a lack of enthusiasm, she said quickly, "Oh, any place, any place at all."

Her mother nodded briskly. "Well, I'm sure your father has something in mind."

Jane's father had something very definite in mind. He shepherded them into what her mother described as a "smart little Italian restaurant." It was little, all right. Jane could scarcely find room for her feet under the table. Her father and mother ate heartily of veal scaloppini and *insalata di spinace,* which turned out to be nothing more than a salad made of spinach; for dessert they had something called "fried cream." Jane would have preferred a hamburger and a chocolate malted.

She twisted one leg around the other, wondering when they would start home. But after dinner, her father drove over the bridge to the new theater. For the first time in her life, Jane wished her parents hadn't taken her with them.

It was eleven o'clock when their front door closed behind the Taylors. Jane rushed to the telephone while her mother stood in the hallway, her purse under one arm, checking through the day's mail.

"Jane!" Mrs. Taylor called.

Jane put the telephone down. "Yes?"

"Do you know you have a library book that's overdue?"

"I have?" Jane went into the hall and took the card from her mother's hand. She read the printed notice.

"They've made a mistake," she said promptly. "I returned it. That is, Merilee returned it for me."

She went to the telephone and dialed Merilee's number. "May I speak to Merilee, please?"

"At eleven o'clock?" It was Mr. Kennedy and obviously he was annoyed.

Jane glanced at the kitchen clock. She hadn't given any thought to the hour. "Oh, is she asleep? I'm sorry."

"Just a minute," Mr. Kennedy snapped. She heard Merilee calling in the background.

"Hello?" It was Merilee.

"It's Jane."

"Oh, hello, Jane." Merilee yawned. "I was just going to bed."

Jane looked at the card in her hand. "Merilee, you returned that library book of mine, didn't you? I got a card from the library and I was sure it was a mis—"

"Oh, gosh!" said Merilee. "I forgot all about it. I'll return it tomorrow."

"The fine is ten cents," said Jane, reading the card.

Merilee yawned again. "I'll pay it—tomorrow."

Jane hung up. Her mother came into the kitchen.

"Good heavens, you're not going to start phoning at this hour are you?"

Jane sighed. "No," she said, "I guess not." But she looked at the telephone yearningly. She had so many calls to make.

She went upstairs and took the dress out of the box. She held it in front of her as she stood before the long mirror. It was really a beautiful dress. Then she looked at herself blankly in the mirror. She had forgotten—absolutely forgotten—to tell Merilee about the new formal when she had telephoned her. Merilee would love the dress. She would absolutely love it.

She swung the dress in front of the mirror and tried to imagine herself wearing it with the pink slippers. She half-closed her eyes to get the effect. "Perfect!" she said aloud. "Just perfect."

Then she hung the dress in her closet, undressed, and got into bed. But she jumped out again to get a pencil and some of her note paper; she took these back to bed with her. She wrote down the names of all of the people she could think of, who might possibly need a baby-sitter in the next two weeks.

Jane fell asleep with the pencil in her hand.

The next week flew by. The telephone calls Jane made the next morning netted her three short baby-sitting jobs. Each day she counted her money, then she telephoned other prospects.

She went to Mount Rainier one day with the Stevensons, to keep little Tommy happy in the back seat so that his parents could enjoy the ride. She stayed overnight with the Laskys' baby when his parents went to a wedding in Vancouver. She even washed dishes for Mrs. Evans one afternoon while she was having her hair done. But Jane still was five dollars from her goal on the Wednesday before Judy's party.

After counting and recounting the money, she pushed it to the back of her top drawer and sat thoughtfully on the bed. Suddenly she jumped. She hadn't found a substitute for Mrs. Almvig!

Startled, she looked at herself in the mirror. She had been so busy phoning for baby-sitting jobs and fulfilling them that the Saturday night job for Mrs. Almvig had slipped completely out of her mind.

Jane ran downstairs so fast that she tripped on the bottom step and fell to her knees. Her mother was in the kitchen, peeling potatoes for dinner. Jane blurted out her problem.

"Why, Jane," Mrs. Taylor said, "I thought you had taken care of that long ago!"

"I forgot," said Jane hurriedly as she dialed a number. "Is it a crime to forget?" she asked, seeing the frown on her mother's face. But she bent her head over the phone, ashamed of her outburst for she knew that she was really angry with herself, not her mother.

"Hello, is that you, Anita?" she said breathlessly into the telephone.

Anita listened to her request, before saying, "But I'm going to Judy Anderson's party. I wouldn't miss it for anything in the world. Why, next to the club dance, it's going to be about the most important social function of the summer. I've heard they're having everything catered! Can you imagine!"

Jane tried Carol Garland.

"Oh, Jane!" shrieked Carol. "Do you mean your mother's making you baby-sit instead of letting you go to Judy's party. I'd die. I'd absolutely die. Her mother told my mother that Judy's been on the phone night and day. She's inviting almost everyone in our class. Isn't that something?"

Jane hung up, and looked at her mother. "Judy's inviting almost everyone in our class," she said tragically.

She continued to telephone. She called Trudy Nelson. "It's turning into the most exciting party I ever heard of. I hear they are even having more boys than girls!" Trudy shrilled.

Jane's hand shook as she dialed the next number.

"Is that you, Jane? I just saw a truck drive up to Judy's house with a whole raft of Japanese lanterns. Oh, I can't wait for Saturday night. Can you?"

Jane didn't say anything.

"What did you call me about, Jane?"

"Oh, nothing. Nothing very much."

Jane wouldn't give up. She called everyone she could think of. Girls she hadn't seen in years. She even called Gladys Allen, and she didn't really know Gladys. She had bumped into her once at school and had stopped to pick up the books that had fallen to the floor.

Gladys let her voice drop to a whisper. "It's all a plot," she said, "a plan to get the boys to ask us younger girls to the club dance. Judy's mother figured it out. Judy's mother says that it's just a matter of getting the boys and girls together at the proper time."

Jane replaced the telephone. She knew what she had to do. Hastily she dialed another number.

"Hello!" she said. Her voice was firm, determined. "Mrs. Almvig? This is Jane. About Saturday night," she began.

"Oh, Jane," Mrs. Almvig interrupted her. "I was just about to call you. Seven o'clock on Saturday will be all right. We're going out for dinner," she confided, as if she were another girl. "It's our anniversary. Our fifth anniversary. And for a while I almost thought we weren't going

41

to make it. Johnny had a slight fever, and here these friends were coming all the way from Spokane and— Well, I'm so relieved. All you have to remember to do is to give him his medicine when he coughs. 'As long as it's Jane,' I told the doctor, 'I won't have a moment's worry.'"

Jane cleared her throat.

"Thank you for checking with me, dear," said Mrs. Almvig. "Good-by."

Jane looked at the telephone. "Good-by," she said hoarsely, and hung up. She turned and stared at her mother.

"I couldn't," said Jane. "I guess I just couldn't."

Her mother seemed to have come to a decision. She spoke rapidly. "I have been talking with your father, and it seems that something has come up and he won't be able to take me with him Saturday." She took a breath. "And really I see no reason why I shouldn't go over and sit with little Johnny while you go to the party. After all," she said lightly, "I can knit over there just as well as I can here."

Jane jumped up. "Oh, Mother!" she cried. "Oh, Mother, would you?"

Her father was standing in the doorway with a look of amazement on his face. "What's all this about?" he asked.

Mrs. Taylor shook her head. "Now, Jane, why don't you call Judy Anderson and tell her you'll go to her party?"

Jane dialed the number. "Judy? Jane. I can come to your party."

"Oh, Jane, I'm so glad," said Judy. "Someone told me that maybe you'd have to baby-sit."

"No," said Jane, "that's all fixed."

"Good. Oh, Jane?"

"Yes?"

"Everybody's decided not to dress up. Just cotton dresses or skirts and blouses. My mother thought it would be more fun that way."

"Oh," said Jane. She hung up.

Her mother picked the broom up and began to sweep the floor.

"Mother," Jane's voice was small and weak. "Do you think Davis's will take the dress back?"

Her mother turned slowly. "Take the dress back?"

Jane nodded. "They're not wearing formals to this party. I guess most of the girls want to save theirs for the club dance."

Mrs. Taylor said lightly, "Oh, I don't think there's any need to take it back. It's such a pretty dress, and— Well, I'm sure there'll be some other party where you can wear it."

She means the club dance, thought Jane. She thinks maybe someone will ask me to the club dance. In spite of herself, her spirits lifted.

CHAPTER FOUR

Jane rinsed her hair three times, pulling at each strand to make sure it squeaked. When hair squeaks it's clean, she'd always heard. Satisfied as to its cleanliness, she wrapped her hair in a towel, opened the bathroom door, and listened to the sounds from downstairs.

Her mother was in the den, talking to the parakeet. Jane tiptoed down the stairs and into the kitchen. She opened the refrigerator and searched among the fruit and vegetables for a lemon. Finding one, she dropped it into the pocket of her robe and then, on an impulse, she took an egg before she closed the refrigerator door. All the starlets used egg facials to look their best, Jane had read, and this was certainly the time to look her best. But she wasn't sure that her mother would approve of a facial, so she decided not to say anything about it.

The telephone rang. Jane reached for it quickly. The pulse at the base of her throat began to beat rapidly.

"Hello?" It was Merilee. "Jane?"

"Oh, Merilee!" Jane's voice was as gay as she could

make it. She hadn't told Merilee about her formal. She didn't know why, but she hadn't told her best friend. Of course, she'd been so busy, looking for jobs as a baby-sitter—

Merilee said, "Charlotte told me you're going to Judy's party."

Jane nodded.

Merilee went on, as if she had seen the nod. "Well, wait for me tonight," she commanded. "I'll walk over to the Andersons with you. And Jane—" Merilee giggled.

"Yes?"

Merilee's voice dropped to a whisper. "Keep your fingers crossed," she said.

Jane smiled at the telephone. "Oh, I will," she answered in a fervent whisper. "I certainly will!"

She hummed a little as she went upstairs. Merilee, she was sure, would be invited to the club dance. As for her-self—she took a deep breath and raised both hands with her fingers crossed.

In the bathroom, Jane filled the washbowl with tepid water and squeezed the lemon into it. She swished the water through her hair.

"It's just to bring out the high lights," she said to her-self. She liked the expression "high lights." Merilee's hair had high lights; Jane wasn't sure whether her own hair had, but it certainly would pay to encourage any tendency to brightness.

She wrapped the towel around her head again and looked hesitantly at the egg. Her mother didn't approve of

Jane's putting "stuff" on her face. But this, after all, was only an egg.

Quickly she picked up the egg and tapped it against the water glass. She let the yolk slip down the drain, and caught the white in the glass. She dipped a piece of cotton into the egg white, and applied some of it to her forehead, her nose, and her chin. She could feel her skin stiffen as the egg white dried. Jane breathed a satisfied sigh. This was just what was supposed to happen, according to the magazine article; she sat on the edge of the bathtub and closed her eyes. A few minutes later she heard her mother's step on the stairs. She opened her eyes, jumped up, and locked the door.

"Jane?"

"I'm here, Mother, doing my hair," she called. Her face felt as if it were made of cardboard. She bent over the washbowl and splashed water on her forehead, nose, and chin. Experimentally she opened and closed her mouth. Her face still felt stiff. She took the washcloth and soap, and scrubbed it vigorously.

Jane inspected herself in the mirror. Except for a slight pinkish cast, her skin didn't look any different. "It probably takes time to work," she told herself. The next time she would leave the egg white on longer.

Her mother had stopped outside the bathroom door. "I'm finishing some ironing," she said. "If you'll tell me which blouse and skirt you've decided to wear, I can give them a quick pressing for you."

Jane hesitated. "I'll let you know in a few minutes," she replied.

"But I'm finishing the ironing now," said Mrs. Taylor.

Jane looked in the mirror again. "Maybe the pink one," she called. When she saw that the pinkish hue of her skin hadn't faded she said quickly, "No! I guess maybe the blue-striped skirt." Then she remembered there was a tear in the blue skirt. "Oh, no!" she said. "Oh, gee, Mother, can't you wait?"

She heard her mother sigh.

"I mean, I can't decide yet, and I can iron it myself anyway."

"All right," said her mother, "but I think the pink skirt would be better."

Jane frowned at her reflection in the mirror. Her mother, she knew, was still standing in the hall. She wished her mother wouldn't try to help her so much; she wished she could say so without being rude. She heard her mother sigh again and go down the hall.

Jane turned back to the mirror, wondering if she dared to pluck a few stray hairs from her eyebrows. She found her mother's tweezers in the medicine cabinet and poised them over her left eye. Closing her eye she plucked one hair from her eyebrows.

"Ouch!" she exclaimed involuntarily. She looked into the mirror. There was a pin point of red where the hair had been plucked. Jane rubbed at it, and returned the tweezers to the cabinet. Some girls, she decided, look better with thick eyebrows.

She began to set her hair. She combed it and fluffed it and tried it this way and that. She trimmed the bangs and put the ends up in pin-curls. She was doing the last pin-curl when she heard her father coming up the stairs.

"I'm in here, Daddy," she shouted.

"Jane!" Mrs. Taylor called sharply from downstairs. "Get out of the bathroom. My goodness, you've been in there all afternoon."

Quickly Jane gathered up the wet towels and dropped them into the hamper. She opened the door. "I haven't either!" she felt impelled to retort. Passing her parents' room, she paused to say, "I'm out of the bathroom, Daddy."

"Hi, baby!" her father said, coming to the door. He looked at her questioningly.

"I'm going to a party!" she explained.

"Oh, the party!"

"Wait till you see my hair," she said. .

"Well, I'll do that," he said with an affectionate smile.

Jane turned away. "I must press my skirt," she said vaguely. There was something she had forgotten, something about this evening. What was it?

In her room, she went slowly to the closet and contemplated the clothes before her. She took out the white formal and regarded it wistfully. Then she replaced it carefully on its hanger. Sighing, Jane pulled out the pink skirt and held it up. "Well, it'll have to do," she said. "I guess it'll have to do." She tossed the skirt over her arm, found the blouse that went with it, and hurried downstairs.

Her father stopped in the kitchen a few minutes later, on his way to the garage. "Shall I drop you off at your party on my way?" he asked.

Jane shook her head. "No, Daddy, the party doesn't begin until eight-thirty. Mother and I are going to have supper first. Merilee is stopping by for me," she added importantly. "We're going to Judy's together."

Her father kissed her. "Well, good-by. Have a good time."

She laughed at his serious expression. "Oh, I will," she said. "I certainly will."

Her mother hurried into the room. "Why, Jane, you haven't pressed your skirt. The ironing board's in my way. I must fix our supper."

"Well," said Mr. Taylor, "I must get going. Sorry I can't give either of you a lift."

Mrs. Taylor laughed. "It's only around the corner. Remember me to Mr. Olson," she added.

"I will. Good-by." Mr. Taylor kissed his wife.

The telephone rang just as Jane and her mother were finishing supper. It was Merilee.

"Jane? Are you almost ready?"

Jane put her hand up to the pin-curls on her head. "Well, almost," she said.

Her mother looked up from the ironing board where she was pressing the pink skirt.

"That is, I will be in just a few minutes."

"Okay," said Merilee. "I'll be there in a few minutes."

"That was Merilee," said Jane as she turned from the telephone. She saw the expression on her mother's face tighten, but she pretended not to notice it.

"She's coming right over," she said.

49

Her mother pressed down hard on the iron. "There," she said, "that's done."

Jane opened her mouth. She felt she should say something. Something in defense of Merilee.

"Merilee is going to have *two* formals," she said, as if that proved something. Then gathering up her pink skirt and blouse, she rushed up the stairs.

She was almost dressed when her mother called to her. "I'm leaving now. Have a good time, dear."

Jane went to the head of the stairs and looked down at her mother. "Good-by." She leaned over the banister. "And thank you, Mother."

Her mother opened the front door and waved to her. "Come home right after the party!" she called gaily. "And be sure to have someone walk home with you."

"Oh, I will," Jane promised. She went back to her room to get her sweater and lipstick.

Downstairs she waited for Merilee, her sweater over her shoulders and her lipstick secure in her pocket.

Jane stood in the hall, tapping her foot on the floor. Then she walked into the living room and looked at herself in the mirror above the fireplace. The house seemed so quiet. She went into the kitchen to look at the clock. Returning to the hall, she opened the front door, so that she could hear Merilee's step, and ran swiftly upstairs. Rummaging in her top drawer, she found the eyelash curler she had hidden there; leaning close to the mirror, she clamped it on the lashes of her right, then her left eye. She put the curler at the back of the drawer again, and walked slowly downstairs.

Again she listened for Merilee's step on the sidewalk. But there was no sound except the shrill chatter of the parakeet in the den. Impulsively she ran across the hall and closed the door to her father's den.

Jane went into the kitchen again and looked at the clock. Dismayed, she saw that thirty minutes had passed since Merilee's phone call. Judy's party would be starting!

Jane grabbed the telephone and dialed Merilee's number. The phone rang and rang. She hung up and dialed again, just to be sure she had rung the right number. This time there was an immediate answer.

"Hello?" It was Merilee's oldest brother.

Jane tried to keep the nervousness from her voice. "Has Merilee left?"

"Who is this?"

"This is Jane Taylor. Has Merilee left yet?"

"Sure she has." His tone was brash.

"Well, how long ago?" she persisted.

There was a pause. Then— "Maybe twenty minutes or half an hour. I dunno."

Merilee lived only two blocks away. "Do you know whether she was coming to my house?"

"I dunno," he repeated. "Some boy stopped by and she went to a party. Are you having a party?"

Jane looked at the telephone. "Thank you," she said hollowly, and hung up.

Hadn't Merilee remembered her promise to stop by for Jane? Remember. "Remember me to Mr. Olson," Mother had said to Dad. That was what Jane had been trying to recall this afternoon.

Mr. Olson was coming from somewhere out of town and her father was taking him to dinner. "I'll wear my new black," her mother had said when the plan was first discussed. And she had bought the white gloves— Her mother had given up the dinner to sit with little Johnny Almvig. She'd given it up so that Jane could go to Judy's party, and the sacrifice was in vain, because Jane wasn't going to the party. "Oh, no!" she groaned.

The telephone rang. She picked it up slowly.

"Jane? This is Merilee."

"Merilee! I've been waiting and waiting! Where are you?"

Merilee's voice dropped to a whisper. "I'm at Judy's."

"But—"

"You see," said Merilee, "Woody stopped by to pick me up just as I was leaving. And— Well, I couldn't very well tell him I had to stop by for you, could I?"

When Merilee said it, it sounded reasonable enough.

"No, I guess not," said Jane dully.

"You'd better come right over," said Merilee. "Everybody's here."

Jane hung up. She walked quickly down the hall and through the front door. She didn't know why she was walking so fast; in no time at all she stood in front of Judy's house. Reluctantly she turned up the walk. At the steps she hesitated, then tiptoed up to the porch.

The porch lights were burning and Japanese lanterns

swayed from the ceiling. Sounds of music, gay voices, and laughter floated through the windows.

Jane couldn't see the doorbell; she knocked timidly on the door. Then she made herself knock more loudly. It seemed an interminable time before the door opened.

CHAPTER FIVE

"Oh, Jane!" Judy cried, opening the door wide. "I'm so glad you could come."

Jane stepped inside. She looked around her hastily, pretending not to see Merilee waving wildly from across the living room. Quietly she made her way up the stairs to Judy's room where the girls had left their wraps.

Merilee followed her, rushing into the room just as Jane dropped her sweater on the bed. Merilee pounced on her, throwing her arms around her and hugging her tightly. She didn't seem to notice Jane's lack of warmth.

"I've been asked!" Merilee exulted. "I've just been asked to the club dance!"

Jane looked at her. Merilee's lipstick was much too bright, she noticed, and Merilee was actually wearing mascara on her eyelashes!

"Oh, I could just die!" Merilee gushed. "I could just die right here!"

"That's nice," Jane said automatically. To her own ears her voice sounded strangely like her mother's.

Merilee darted a glance at her. Then she shrugged and said, "Well, I'd better get back. I told him I'd just be a minute." She pranced from the room.

Jane looked at herself in the mirror. Merilee hadn't *said* it was Woody who had invited her to the dance. But who else could it be? Hadn't Woody called for Merilee tonight? The thought made Jane's throat feel dry, and she unfastened, then fastened the top button of her blouse. She heard Judy calling her.

"Jane! Hurry up. We're going to draw numbers for the next dance."

"I'm coming!" said Jane. Her voice sounded hoarse.

She cleared her throat, glanced uncertainly at herself once more in the mirror, fixed a smile on her face, and hurried down the stairs. Judy met her, holding out two slips of paper.

"Here, Jane," she said. "You choose."

Jane took the one nearer to her. She looked at it, but the number on the paper told her nothing.

"Come on," said Judy, "we have to match our numbers with the boys'."

Judy whirled away and Jane reluctantly followed her into the living room. She held the slip of paper in her hand. Someone bumped into her and she stepped aside hurriedly, pulling her elbows in. Everybody seemed to be finding partners quickly. Jane looked at her number again, then glanced about the room. Her heart pounded. Woody was standing alone. Jane straightened her back, and raised her scrap of paper in a half-wave. But Woody had turned away; he was comparing his number with that of a girl who stood beside him. Then he threw the paper over his shoulder.

Jane's arm fell limply to her side and the paper in her fingers fluttered to the floor. She stooped to retrieve it.

"Hey!" said a low voice. She looked up. "Haven't we got the same number?" The voice cracked.

Jane stood up. She smiled stiffly and held out the slip. The boy took the paper. He looked at it carefully. He compared it with his own. Then he looked at Jane and back to the numbers. Jane felt herself reddening.

"I guess they're the same," he said, holding out the slips for Jane to see. "I didn't wear my glasses," he went on, apologetically. "My sister says I look better without my specs. But, honestly, I can't see a thing."

Jane laughed. "Maybe I'd better lead you around," she said. "I've had quite a bit of experience leading the ponies around at the park."

"Hey!" he said. "I've been called an owl, but never a horse!"

It was easy to laugh again. The boy held out his hand and confidently Jane led him out to the middle of the floor. They were halfway through the dance when it occurred to her that *he* might ask her to the club dance. She missed a step.

"Sorry," the boy muttered.

"My fault," Jane replied. She gritted her teeth, determined not to step on his foot again. And, of course, she did.

"Pardon me," he said politely.

The music stopped. Jane tried to think of something interesting to say.

"Well, thank you," her partner said. Looking over her shoulder, he took a quick side step. "Hey, Judy!" he shouted, and plunged toward his hostess.

Jane went to stand against the wall. She drifted carefully from one wall to the other during the next dances, so that she wouldn't be seen standing in one place too long. Then, after a while, she stood on the edge of a little group of girls and pretended to be listening to the music.

She glanced across the room where a few boys stood, looking as if they wanted to dance with someone who was already dancing. Among them, casually tapping his feet to the music, was Woody. Their eyes met for a brief moment before Jane hastily looked away, but not before she had seen Woody take a tentative step toward her. Her heart beat furiously. Maybe Woody was going to ask her to dance!

But she never found out, for suddenly the record ended and the very next moment Judy's mother came out of the kitchen from the door behind Jane. She smiled at the girls.

"Now why don't you girls who don't care to dance start passing sandwiches?" she asked brightly.

The party wasn't "catered" after all. Jane blinked. Then she nodded politely and followed Mrs. Anderson into the kitchen.

"Well, Jane, for a moment I didn't recognize you. It's the hair-do!" Mrs. Anderson pronounced.

Jane went to stand against the wall.

Jane's hand went up to touch her bangs.

"It's very becoming, Jane; most becoming."

Jane smiled. "What can I do to help?" Without being told, she was already stacking sandwiches on a tray.

"That's right," Mrs. Anderson approved. "How's your mother, Jane?"

"Oh, fine," said Jane. "Shall I fill the other tray, too?"

"Do that," Mrs. Anderson nodded.

She went to the table and showed the other girls how to fill the punch glasses. Then she came back to Jane.

"Judy speaks of you often, Jane," she said warmly. "She thinks you're the smartest girl in her class, and says that you draw beautifully."

Jane shrugged. "I guess things like *that* are easy for me." She didn't try to keep the bitterness from her voice.

Mrs. Anderson looked at her searchingly. "You're going to the club dance, Jane." It was half a question, half a statement.

Jane stared at the sandwiches. "Well, no—I guess not," she said, and blushed.

Mrs. Anderson's hands paused in mid-air, then quickly continued to count paper napkins. She looked at Jane conspiratorially.

"Most of these boys would give a month's allowance to go to the club dance," she said softly. "But boys of this age are so shy."

Jane raised her head. She hadn't noticed that.

"You have to encourage them a little, dear," said Judy's mother. "You know."

Jane nodded. But she was not at all sure that she did know.

Mrs. Anderson put her head close to Jane's. "I'm going to announce girls' choice for the last dance," she whispered. "Why don't you stand next to some nice boy, and ask him to dance? Be interested in what he talks about while you're dancing." She nodded her head emphatically.

Jane nodded, too. Suddenly she felt hopeful.

Judy and Charlotte came into the kitchen then, to ask if the refreshments were ready. Before the door closed behind them, someone turned off the lights in the living room. There was a burst of laughter, followed by silence.

"Let's get in there quickly and get their minds on the food," said Mrs. Anderson, handing Jane a tray.

Jane put her shoulder to the swinging door and pushed. She faced the darkened room. Someone whispered a warning; a girl giggled. Jane could guess why some boy had turned the lights out.

"Hey, who's that?" a masculine voice demanded.

Another voice answered carelessly, "Oh, it's only Jane."

Someone laughed shortly. Jane tried to swallow the lump in her throat. She stood clutching the tray, while her heart beat painfully.

Only Jane! Not a girl to be called for on the way to a party. Not a girl to be kissed in the dark, or even one to be invited to dance. Only unimportant Jane Taylor!

The lights went on. "Isn't this a marvelous party?" someone asked.

"Marvelous," Jane answered mechanically. She knew that her smile was strained; her face felt stiff.

The stiffness seemed to spread from her face to her hands and feet. She danced once more, because Judy's mother was watching her. When it was girls' choice, Jane asked Hank Cooke who stood nearest to her. But she danced awkwardly, she didn't hear the music, and she could think of nothing to say.

When the party ended, there was a general scramble for wraps. Jane, with her sweater over her shoulders, suddenly wondered how she was to get home. Her mother didn't allow her to walk alone at night, and she had promised that she would come home with someone. But she wasn't going to ask to walk with Merilee—not for a hundred dollars!

Merilee obviously had no intention of walking home with her. Out of the corner of her eye, Jane saw her laughing with a group of boys. Woody, who had stopped to call for Merilee, would walk her home of course.

But Judy's mother stood, like a sentinel, at the door. "Is your father calling for you, dear?" she asked as Jane tried to slip past her after mumbling her thanks.

"Oh, no," said Jane; then she could have bitten her tongue.

"Well, why don't you walk with Woody and Barry. Woody!" Mrs. Anderson called.

Jane looked at the floor.

"You live near Jane, don't you, Woody? Will you see that she gets home?" Mrs. Anderson's tone was that dreadful one mothers use when they trample on one's innermost feelings.

"Sure. I guess so," Woody said without enthusiasm.

"Oh, no," Jane protested; but it was only a whisper. "Thank you, Mrs. Anderson," she managed to say, "but I made arrangements with Merilee."

It wasn't a lie, she told herself fiercely. She *had* made arrangements with Merilee—to walk to the party.

Judy's mother looked around for Merilee. "But I thought she—"

At that moment Merilee reappeared. She came running down from the second floor. Jane shrank back against the wall.

"Oh, there you are, Merilee," Mrs. Anderson said. "We were looking for you. Jane has an invitation to walk home with Woody and Barry, but it seems she had already made arrangements with you."

Jane stared unbelievingly at Mrs. Anderson. Why, it wasn't that way at all. But Merilee glanced at Woody and Barry who were waiting awkwardly. "Well, why don't we all walk home together?" she said.

With a light laugh that Jane couldn't help admiring, Merilee thrust one hand through Jane's arm and the other through Woody's. (Then it *was* Woody who had asked Merilee to the club dance.) Barry walked on the other side of Woody.

They walked four abreast down the dark street. After a short silence, Merilee murmured, "Only six weeks until the dance!"

Merilee chattered on, and the boys guffawed, but Jane

hardly heard them. Her heart had warmed toward her friend. Merilee, she decided, hadn't done anything so terrible in not calling for her on the way to Judy's party. She could see just how it was. After all, she couldn't expect Merilee to tell Woody that *she* had to call for Jane. That would have been awkward. Merilee was still her best friend. She squeezed her arm.

But Jane was dreading the moment when they would come to the Kennedys' where Merilee would leave them, and she would have to walk on with the boys. She tried to think of something to say. But when they came to her house, Merilee didn't stop.

"I'll walk on to Jane's with you," she announced to the boys, "and you'll just have to walk me back again." Her tone made it sound as if she were conferring a great favor.

"Well, hear that!" exclaimed Barry in mock indignation.

"Huh!" said Woody. "Do you think we're going to walk back and forth all night?"

They walked on until they were in front of the Taylors' house. Quickly Jane said good night, and ran up the walk to the porch. She closed the front door behind her and took a deep breath.

Her mother came into the hall from the living room. She looked at Jane expectantly. "How was the party?" she asked.

With an effort, Jane managed to yawn before she replied. "All right," she said.

"Oh," her mother said.

Jane went upstairs. In her bedroom, she opened the

closet door and looked at the white formal on its hanger. She knew with certainty that she would never wear it. She closed the closet door and tried to shut the vision of the dress from her mind.

Jane didn't brush her hair or even wash her face. She put on her oldest pajamas, got into bed, and closed her eyes. Hot tears ran down her cheeks.

CHAPTER SIX

When Jane awoke the next morning, she decided she would put Judy's party out of her mind. It was over and done with as far as she was concerned. She would think no more about it.

In the bathroom, she passed a comb hastily through her hair and washed her face without looking in the mirror. She went down to the kitchen. Her father was reading the Sunday paper at the breakfast table.

"Well, how did the party go?" he asked jovially.

Jane picked up her orange juice and made quite a show of drinking it. "Fine," she said, wiping her mouth on the pink paper napkin.

Her mother hummed as she turned the pancakes. Jane looked at her quickly. Her mother always hummed that way when she was worried about something. But what could her mother possibly have to worry about this morning? Jane poured herself a glass of milk.

"Anybody going to church this morning?" asked her father.

"We're *all* going to church this morning," Mrs. Taylor said firmly.

Jane smiled weakly. Every Sunday morning her father asked the same question, and every Sunday morning her mother gave him the same answer. Usually it never failed to amuse Jane. But this morning it didn't seem funny at all.

"If you don't mind," she said, "I think I'll skip church today."

Her father looked at her mother. There was a short silence. Then Mr. Taylor said plaintively, "Do you mean I have to go if she doesn't? Now do you call that fair?"

"You weren't out 'partying' last night," Jane's mother said briskly. "However, we're all late for breakfast this morning, so I propose that we eat, stack the dishes to be washed later, and *all* be ready to leave for church in forty-five minutes."

Jane sighed. But she was ready when her parents were, and she walked docilely down the street between them. She listened to the sermon, looking neither to the right nor to the left, and she didn't hear one word of it.

Sunday dinner was a quiet one. Stolidly Jane ate through the soup, the roast beef and the mashed potatoes, the salad, and didn't even hesitate at the dessert. She would never wear the formal anyway, so what difference did it make if she gained a ton?

Mr. Taylor discussed with his wife the matter of trimming the blackberry bushes behind the garage. Jane listened with only half an ear. Silently she dried the dishes for her mother.

"There," said her mother, shutting the cupboard, "that's that."

Jane folded the dish towel. "Mother," she said, "do you think I'm too *serious?*"

Her mother hesitated. "Well, Jane," she replied slowly, "I think seriousness can be a *good* quality. When seriousness means"—she seemed to search for the right words—"being responsible, or rather taking responsibility, then to be serious is a very good thing."

Jane frowned. Her mother didn't know what she meant.

"No," Mrs. Taylor went on, "I don't think you are too serious. But I do think you are apt to—well, worry about little things too much." She patted Jane's hand. "You are prone to take things too much to heart."

Jane raised her head. She waited for her mother to come to the point.

"But that's perfectly natural for someone of your age. You are growing up, Jane. Learning to take things in stride is a matter of maturing. After all, you're only fifteen!

"Always be yourself, Jane," her mother added. "Be true to the best that's in yourself. Always. Other things will fall into place as you grow older."

Jane nodded. But she was almost sorry she had tried to talk with her mother. Her mother hadn't understood the meaning of her question. What Jane wanted to know was whether her seriousness made her unpopular with boys. And her mother had spoken to her as if she were a child attempting her first steps. Jane shrugged. Firmly she changed the subject.

"I think I'll walk to the park, and watch the ponies."

"Good idea," said her mother, picking up her knitting.

Jane hurried past Merilee's house. She remembered the walk home from the party last night, and she blushed to think of it. Somehow the whole evening had resulted to her discredit and she wasn't ready to face Merilee.

Jane stopped suddenly. She was directly in front of Judy Anderson's house. On an impulse she turned up the walk, ran lightly up the porch steps, and knocked at the door.

Mrs. Anderson answered the door. "Why, hello, Jane," she said warmly.

Jane smiled her greeting. It was strange how like Judy Mrs. Anderson sounded.

"Is Judy home?" asked Jane, a little breathlessly. She had never sought out Judy before.

Mrs. Anderson opened the door wider. "She certainly is." She smiled at Jane. "Some of the young men who were at the party stopped by to say hello and they are all out in the kitchen looking for Cokes. Judy will be so glad that you came. Come right in."

Jane took a quick step backward. "Oh! Well, I can't stop now," she said hurriedly. "I only wanted to tell her what a nice party it was, and—"

She turned and started down the porch steps. "Well, I'll phone her later," she said.

"But Jane—" Mrs. Anderson called after her.

Jane made quite a show of looking at her watch. "I really must run," she said.

And she did. She ran all the way to the park entrance before she stopped. She looked at her watch. It had stopped at a quarter to twelve. She had forgotten to wind it. Jane looked at it for a long time, biting her lip.

She felt a little ashamed of herself. It wouldn't have hurt her to go in and say hello to Judy, even if those boys were there. She walked hastily into the park.

The trouble with her, Jane reflected, was that she had no self-confidence. Then she made a wry face. No wonder she had no self-confidence.

"Only Jane!" She could hear the careless voice again. "Only Jane."

She broke into a run; she ran past the rose garden and the children's wading pool and the new ape house. She ran to the little corral at the far end of the park where the ponies were slowly trotting around and around, with little boys and girls on their backs.

Jane sat on the fence and watched them. She'd always loved to sit here and watch the ponies. But today it didn't seem like fun at all.

"Kid stuff!" she whispered to herself.

What she really wanted to do was to go to the riding stable and take Bonny out on the trail. She would ride and ride—until night came. There was no reason why she shouldn't. It wasn't as if she had to save her money for something.

"Only Jane. Only Jane. Only Jane." The words went

through her mind relentlessly. She shook her head and slid from the fence.

Slowly she made her way back past the ape house and the wading pool. She walked through the maze of paths in the rose garden. The fragrance of the roses filled the air and she breathed deeply of it. Of all the flowers in the park, she liked the roses best, even better than the orchids in the greenhouse.

Suddenly Jane realized that she was hungry. She decided to go home.

As she passed the Kennedys' house, Merilee bounced out the front door.

"Jane!" she called. "Oh, Jane, wait a minute."

Jane stopped. "Well, hi!" she said.

Merilee came down the path to the sidewalk looking at her a little curiously, Jane thought.

"Gee, Jane, I'm really sorry . . ."

Why, she's going to apologize for not stopping by for me last night, thought Jane, amazed.

". . . that you didn't get a date for the dance last night at Judy's."

Jane's amazement turned quickly to annoyance. "Oh, for heaven's sake, Merilee," she said. "It isn't that *serious*." She stressed the word, and felt that somehow she had righted herself.

Merilee looked at her a moment; then she shrugged lightly. "Well, maybe it isn't," she agreed.

Impulsively Jane said, "Really, I'm awfully glad Woody asked you."

A pleased expression came over Merilee's face, to be

quickly displaced by a frown of concern. She said, "Really, it's just too bad that you—"

Jane interrupted her. "Oh, forget it, Merilee."

She walked on down the street. She turned to wave when she came to the corner, and Merilee waved back.

But when she reached the security of her own room, Jane admitted to herself that she might have fooled Merilee, but she hadn't fooled herself. For, no matter how reasonably she tried to view it, not being invited to the club dance was serious. It was perhaps the most serious thing that had happened to her, next to not receiving a horse for her birthday.

Jane threw herself across the foot of her bed, taking care to keep her feet off the spread. She wondered if this was to be the pattern of her life. She wondered if all through her life the important things would be the ones that *didn't* happen. A great lump rose in her throat.

The dress, the beautiful white formal, might hang in her closet, unworn, until she was ninety-nine years old. It might—conceivably. She rolled over and closed her eyes.

"I'll leave a note and ask them to bury me in it," she whispered as two large tears, round and warm, trembled on her eyelids.

Jane opened her eyes and looked around the room. Her eyes skimmed over the rumpled pink blouse and skirt, still on the chair where she had flung them last night, and came to rest on the picture of the horse.

Bonny was just such a beautiful little mare, with soft eyes, a proud head, and a shiny coat. Jane loved the way

Bonny trotted down the middle of the road, with head up, legs high, acting for all the world as if there was no one else on the bridle path. She loved the way Bonny would not slow her pace or even blink until she was almost upon the horse ahead of her before she swerved gracefully around it.

Jane looked at the picture and wished again for a horse of her own. Idly she wondered if there wasn't some way she could earn a horse of her own. She sat up quickly and dried her eyes.

Certainly her mother and her father wouldn't refuse her a horse if she earned it herself. Jane got off the bed and went to her bureau. Opening the top drawer, she frowned as she fingered the small pile of nickels and dimes and quarters. Baby-sitting was too slow. She looked around the room; she paced the floor, thinking.

Downstairs the parakeet began to chatter. "Happy birthday, Jane!" it said, "Happy, happy!"

Jane listened. Then she walked downstairs and into the den. "It's not my birthday any more, you crazy bird," she said, poking a finger into the cage. The parakeet sat on its swing perch and cocked its head. Its beady eyes seemed to blink at her.

Jane put her mouth close to the cage. "Hello," she said firmly. "Say 'Hello'!"

But the bird seemed to have a will of its own. "Happy birthday," it responded. "Happy, happy."

"Hel-lo," said Jane. She mouthed it carefully, pausing between each syllable.

"Birthday," said the bird.

"You be careful," she said crossly, "or I'll trade you for a cat!"

Suddenly Jane straightened up. The solution was so simple that she couldn't understand why she hadn't thought of it before. She ran upstairs, walked past the telephone table in the hall, stopped, and walked quickly back again. It was such a splendid idea that she just had to tell someone. She dialed Merilee's number.

"Guess what!" she said breathlessly.

"What?" asked Merilee.

Jane hadn't actually put the idea into words yet, so she listened carefully as she spoke to Merilee. "I'm going to offer my services at the riding stable in exchange for a horse!"

Now that she had described it, the plan seemed even more logical, more workable. There was a silence at the other end of the line.

"Merilee? Did you hear what I said? I said—"

"Yes, I heard you," Merilee replied, and it sounded as if she were stifling a yawn.

"Well?" asked Jane, smiling in anticipation. "What do you think of it?"

"I think it's crazy, that's what I think," said Merilee.

Jane replaced the telephone. She sat for a long moment, pressing her upper teeth against her lower lip. Her plan had already lost its luster.

Then she straightened her shoulders, and marched into her room. The first thing tomorrow morning, she decided, she would go to the Clearmeadow Stables and apply for a job. If they didn't need anyone there, she'd go to the Ring Academy, and if *they* didn't need anyone— Well, she wouldn't give up.

CHAPTER SEVEN

"Now, Jane," said Mrs. Taylor, "if you're going to ride, you'll have to eat more breakfast than that."

Impatiently Jane took another swallow of milk. Then she stood up, tucking her shirt into her jodhpurs. "I want to make the nine-fifteen bus," she said.

"Did you pick up your room?" asked her mother, as if the nine-fifteen bus would wait for Jane.

Hastily she ran up to her room, stuffed her pajamas under her pillow, pulled up the bedspread, and kicked a stray shoe into the closet. She ran downstairs.

"Better take your sweater," her mother called from the kitchen. Jane hesitated, then she ran upstairs, pulled a sweater from a drawer, and ran downstairs again.

The telephone rang. Mrs. Taylor answered it. Jane opened the front door.

"Jane!"

"Yes?" It was hard to keep the impatience from her voice.

"Mrs. Almvig wants to know if you will sit with Johnny tomorrow afternoon."

"Tell her I'll let her know tonight," she called.

Her mother came from the kitchen and looked at her in surprise. "Now really, Jane—" she began.

Jane saw the bus coming down the street. "Please, Mother!" she said. "Just tell her that." She ran to catch the bus.

She made a face at her reflection in the bus window after she had sat down. Why did her mother have to be so difficult sometimes? Jane couldn't very well tell Mrs. Almvig that she would sit with Johnny when she didn't know whether she'd be busy with something else tomorrow afternoon, could she?

She smiled at the window. A boy on the street smiled at her and added a wave. She didn't even know him! Jane turned her face quickly to the front of the bus but, for a moment, a warm glow filled her. The bus had made two more stops before she brought her mind back to her project.

As the bus approached the outskirts of the city, Jane's breathing became more rapid. She wondered whether she should speak to Mr. Otis or to old Jack, the groom. She was still undecided as she walked up the short road from the highway to the gate of the Clearmeadow Stables. When she saw Jack cleaning the water troughs, she walked directly toward him.

"Hi, Jack!" she called.

He looked up. "Good mornin'," he said, and turned off the hose. "Good mornin' for ridin', that is."

Jane nodded. Old Jack said that every morning, she supposed. He had said it every morning she had ever ridden here. If it was afternoon, he merely changed his greeting to "Good afternoon," followed by "Good afternoon for ridin', that is."

Jane handed him her riding money. She had meant to ask him about the job right away, but somehow she didn't quite know how to do it.

"You ridin' today?" he asked, and without counting the money put it into his shirt pocket.

He always did that, too. Jane had always smiled to herself at the way he invariably took her money first and then asked the question. But today she was too busy trying to put her idea into words to smile. She said, experimentally, "My, there certainly is a lot of work around here, isn't there?"

"Nope, not so much," Jack said, wiping his wet hands on his riding breeches.

Jane decided that it would be better to talk to Mr. Otis about the job.

She asked, "May I have Bonny to ride today?"

Jack scratched his head. "Haven't got Bonny any more," he said. "You want Prince?"

"You haven't got Bonny any more!" Jane repeated, astonished. She looked toward Bonny's stall.

"Nope! Had to get rid of her."

"But why?" Jane felt a tightness in her chest.

"Well, to tell you the truth," said Jack, "she was goin' blind."

Jane found that she had to swallow hard.

"Remember how she'd trot down the middle of the road, no matter who was comin'?" Jack asked.

Jane nodded.

"She was slowly goin' blind, and 't was a long time before we knew it."

Jane saw herself combing Bonny and currying her, feeding her carrots. It wouldn't make any difference if she was blind.

"Prince ain't been out for a long time," said Jack. "That who you want, Prince?" He didn't wait for her answer but picked up a saddle and began to stride toward Prince's stall.

Jane ran a little to catch up with him. "Where is Bonny?" she demanded. "Where is Bonny now?"

Jack shrugged. "Don't exactly know," he said.

Jane had a sudden vision of Bonny dead—shot as a useless animal. Or—and the thought made her stumble as she followed Jack to Prince's stall—Bonny had been sent to a slaughterhouse where horse meat was put into cans, to feed dogs and cats. She shuddered. She wanted to know where Bonny was, but she was afraid to know.

"You want Prince?" Jack asked. The horse was already saddled.

Jane nodded; she couldn't trust herself to speak. She realized now that all of her wishes for a horse were wishes to have Bonny for her own.

"Ready?" Jack said.

Jane nodded again and grasped the reins. Prince, she knew, was restless and she wasn't sure she could handle him properly; but she wouldn't tell Jack that. Prince was apt to swing out when mounted. She tightened her grasp on the reins and put her left foot in the stirrup. "Whoa, boy," she said softly. She mounted slowly, keeping a firm hold on the reins.

"Keep firm," said Jack, after she had kept firm.

"I'm going to take the upper trail," Jane said.

Jack nodded. "Let him out on the straight stretch," he advised. Then he shook his head. "Business has been purty slow lately. Everybody goin' to the beach, maybe." He scratched his head again.

Jane turned Prince. She remembered to keep her heels down, her elbows in, and her hands low. The upper trail was not the road where she took Bonny. When she came to the straight stretch, she let Prince run. The breeze tore at her hair and was cool on her cheeks. But it was strange to be riding Prince instead of Bonny, and he *was* harder to handle. Jane had no time for thinking, no time to brood on Bonny's fate. But she was almost glad when Prince turned his head toward the stables even though it was a little short of the hour.

"Okay, boy," she said.

There was no use asking if she could work at the Clearmeadow Stables to earn a horse. She didn't want a horse like Prince—or Betsy or even Skyrocket. They were only hacks; they were all right for a ride, but none of them could ever be her friend. The horse she had dreamed of owning was Bonny.

Slowly she rode back, ducking her head to avoid low-hanging branches. Ahead was the stable yard and the white house. As she rode in, Jack was brushing Skyrocket with rhythmic strokes. Jane watched as a car stopped at the gate; its doors opened and three or four children spilled out.

"Can I help? Can I help?" they shrieked as they surrounded Jack.

Not too long ago Jane had been one of those clamoring kids, begging to brush a pony or carry a water pail. She could see that Jack had plenty of help.

Jane turned Prince into the yard and dismounted. Jack came up and patted the horse. "Say," he confided, "I found out where Bonny went."

Jane looked at him quickly. Then she turned her head so that Jack couldn't see the fear in her eyes.

"The boss loaded her on the trailer yesterday and sent her to some nephew of his on a farm. The kid's crazy about horses, he said. Took a shine to Bonny the first day he saw her."

"Thank you!" Jane breathed. "Oh, thank you very much!"

Merilee was right. It had been a crazy idea to think she could earn a horse. Now that Jane considered it, her plan seemed extremely childish. She would put it away in her memory with the childish things that she had relegated to the attic at home, her dolls, her roller skates, her doll carriage. She didn't *need* a horse.

It was almost noon when she flung herself on the bus. She pretended not to see the boy and girl holding hands in the seat across the aisle, and kept her eyes studiously away from the two boys sitting in front of her. Jane sat looking out the window until her neck ached.

She walked slowly from the bus to her house. Her desire to own a horse, it seemed to her, had been nothing but a childish compulsion. In fact, she told herself, as she opened the front door, if someone should appear at this very moment and offer her a horse as a gift— She paused and regarded herself searchingly in the hall mirror. "You know you'd grab it!" she told her reflection.

She grinned at herself and went into the kitchen where her mother was getting lunch.

"Oh there you are, Jane," she said, pouring milk into a glass. "Your Aunt Harriet just called from San Francisco."

Jane took a sip of the milk. "What's Aunt Harriet doing in San Francisco? I thought she lived in Cincinnati."

Mrs. Taylor raised her eyebrows. "My goodness, didn't you even read your birthday card?"

With a sandwich in one hand, Jane opened the drawer under the telephone and fished out the post card. It was a view of the Grand Canyon. She turned it over and read the message. "Congratulations to dear Jane on her fifteenth birthday. Uncle Gordon, Frederick and I are having a wonderful trip. Can't wait to tell you about it."

"Who's Frederick?" she asked. Her Aunt Harriet and Uncle Gordon were childless. Which was a good thing, Jane had often thought; she couldn't imagine how her father and her Aunt Harriet could be brother and sister.

"Frederick," said Mrs. Taylor slowly, as if she were making an important announcement, "is Gordon's brother's son. He's visiting Harriet and Gordon this summer while his parents are in Europe."

Jane giggled. "I can just see Aunt Harriet having to put up with a little kid."

81

Her mother cleared her throat. "Oh, he's not so little," she said in an offhand tone.

Jane set the glass of milk on the table and looked at her mother before she took a bite of her sandwich.

"In fact," Mrs. Taylor went on, "I'd say he's about your age."

Jane swallowed the bite of sandwich she had in her mouth. Her mother went to the sink and began to wash a head of lettuce.

"I understand that Frederick is a very bright boy. On the track team, too, I believe Harriet said." Mrs. Taylor opened a cupboard to take out a bowl. "They're coming to visit us for several days; they'll be here over Labor Day week end."

Jane sat down suddenly on the kitchen stool. Her mother turned to face her.

"It seems to me," she said, "that it would be a good idea for you to reserve that Saturday night and take Frederick to the club dance as your guest. I think it would be the hospitable thing to do."

Jane considered her mother's suggestion and could find nothing wrong with it. "Frederick," she said experimentally. The name had a nice ring to it.

She picked up her glass and took a sip of milk. Her heart began to beat faster as she saw herself in the white formal and the pink slippers.

Jane shrugged. "Okay," she said.

CHAPTER EIGHT

Jane finished her sandwich and drained the glass of milk. She put the glass on the table as carefully as if it had been her mother's best Swedish crystal instead of a jelly glass.

Dreamily she walked from the kitchen into the hall. A ray of sunshine struck the polished banister and Jane realized for the first time how beautiful the staircase was. She floated up the stairs. When she reached the second floor it was if she had climbed to a mountaintop where the atmosphere was so thin and pure it made one light-headed. Jane stood still until the delicious whirling in her head had stopped.

She sat down at the telephone table and propped her head in her hands. A date for the club dance! A grin spread over her face. Quickly she grasped the telephone and dialed Merilee's number. She wondered what Merilee would say when she heard the news.

"Merilee's not home," said one of Merilee's little brothers. "She just went out."

"Thank you," Jane said. She hesitated only a moment before dialing Judy's number.

"Judy?" she said when Judy answered. "It's Jane."

"Well, hi!" Judy sounded pleased.

"I'm going to the club dance," Jane told her.

There was a delighted squeal from the other end of the line. "How wonderful! Oh, Jane, I can't tell you how pleased I am. Barry Mitchell invited me. Who are you going with?"

Jane told it all in a little rush. "Well, his name is Frederick, and he's taking this trip with my aunt and uncle; they're all coming here to visit us over Labor Day. He lives in Cincinnati and he's on the track team at his school. He's not really any relation," she added quickly.

"Jane, he sounds marvelous. The track team! Wonderful!" Then Judy's voice became practical. "I've been looking and looking for a formal and I can't find what I want. Did you get one yet?"

"Go to Davis's," said Jane promptly. "I got the most beautiful dress there."

"I'm coming right over," Judy cried. "I have to see it!"

"I'll be waiting for you," said Jane.

"Just a minute," Judy said. "Someone's at the door."

Jane waited. Then Judy spoke again: "It's Charlotte. She's so excited. She's just had a letter from her cousin and he'll be here over Labor Day and will go to the dance with her. We'll both be over in a minute."

Jane placed the telephone on its cradle. Still smiling, she walked to her room and stood in the doorway. She saw the room suddenly with eyes other than her own.

84

She saw a bed bumpily made, with one edge of the spread dragging on the floor; two bureau drawers were half-open. A pair of stockings lay on her dressing table, and a slip had been flung on the chest of drawers. The waste basket had tipped over, and the closet door was open.

Quickly Jane went to work. She grabbed the slip and stockings and carried them to the clothes hamper in the bathroom. She closed the drawers, righted the waste basket, and threw back the bedspread to straighten the sheets. She had just pulled the spread over the bed again and more or less evened the edges, when the doorbell rang. Jane leaned over the banister.

"I'm up here," she called. "Come on up."

The girls flung themselves on Jane's bed. "Your room is so pretty," Judy said.

Charlotte looked around her. "When I think how my room looks in the middle of the day!" She shuddered.

"Well, you gave me just enough time," Jane laughed.

She picked up a shoe she had missed and threw it in the closet. Then she took out the hanger with the white formal and held it up.

"What do you think?" she asked.

"Oooh!" Charlotte breathed.

"Jane, it's beautiful," said Judy.

Charlotte groaned. "I *am* going to lose weight before the dance. I really am! I'd never fit into a dress like that!"

Jane tried the dress on for them, turning around and around and walking on tiptoe so that they could get the effect.

Judy said, "I saw the sweetest pair of slippers in the window at Langleys'. They would match that rose perfectly."

"Pink, with high heels? Oh, Judy, those are the same slippers I saw. They're just what I want!" Jane cried.

"How lucky can you be?" said Charlotte. "Slippers to match!"

"But my mother says my flats will do very nicely," said Jane, and she made a face.

"Maybe she'll change her mind," Judy said hopefully.

"And maybe she won't," said Jane glumly.

"Oh, well," said Judy, "the important thing is you're going. Frederick." She said the name slowly, rolling it on her tongue. "I think it sounds nice."

"My cousin's name is 'Beetzie,'" said Charlotte, and she shuddered.

Judy bounced on Jane's bed. "Oh Charlotte, stop complaining," she said. "You know you think he's just about the best-looking thing you ever saw!"

"Oh, I'm not complaining," said Charlotte quickly.

"Jane!" Mrs. Taylor called from downstairs. Jane opened her bedroom door.

"Mrs. Anderson just called," said Jane's mother. "She says that Charlotte's mother called her and she wants Judy to come along, too."

"Oh!" exclaimed Charlotte, striking her forehead with her hand. "I forgot! I was supposed to borrow a cup of sugar. I'd better run."

"I'll call you later," Judy said to Jane as she followed Charlotte down the stairs.

Jane looked around her room and smiled. The telephone rang and she stood motionless as she heard her mother answer downstairs.

"Jane."

"Is it for me?" But she was already on the upstairs extension.

"Hello?" she said.

"Hi, Jane; it's Merilee."

They both waited until they heard the click of the downstairs telephone being replaced.

"Did you get the job?" said Merilee.

"What job?" For a moment Jane couldn't think what Merilee was talking about. "Oh! The job. No." Then she giggled. "It was sort of a crazy idea, after all."

Merilee giggled companionably. "Well, you sounded so terribly *serious* about it."

The word hurt. But Jane quickly went on, "You know what?"

"Your father decided to give you a horse, after all," said Merilee.

Jane shrugged with impatience. "Oh, for heaven's sake, Merilee! No!"

"Well then, what?"

Jane took a deep breath. "My aunt and uncle are coming to visit us and they are bringing a boy with them— *he's* no relation—and I'm going to the club dance with him!"

Merilee's reaction was all that Jane could have wished for. "Jane!" she shrieked. "You aren't! You aren't really!"

Jane held the telephone away from her ear, but she listened to Merilee with the pleasure of her friend's astonishment filling her. Then she heard her mother's step on the stairs. Jane turned her head so that her face wouldn't be visible. She said to Merilee, "I'll call you later when we can talk." She replaced the phone on its cradle.

Mrs. Taylor stood in the hall with an armload of clean sheets. "That Judy Anderson is certainly a nice girl," she said.

Jane opened the linen cupboard door; she cleared her throat. "Mother," she said, "what about the pink slippers?"

Her mother was stacking the sheets on the first shelf. She didn't turn her head. "What pink slippers?" she asked absently.

Jane stepped closer to her. "The ones at Langleys'. Remember? I told you they match the rose on my formal perfectly. Don't you think I might—"

"I don't think so," Mrs. Taylor said. She picked up three fresh towels and carried them down the hall to the bathroom.

Jane stood looking at the sheets arranged so neatly in the linen cupboard. She sighed and went back to her room.

She flung herself on her bed and lay with her hands under her head, staring at the ceiling. Then she got up to open the closet door and look at the white dress. She picked up her white flats and held them against the formal.

Jane frowned and threw herself on the bed again. After all, the slippers weren't so important. The important thing was that she was going to the dance.

That's what she told herself that day, and the next day,

and on the one after that. But on Saturday she walked down to Langleys' and looked in the window again. She looked past the row of colored plastics and patent leathers, past silver heels and platform soles. The pink slippers were gone! Jane looked again. Carefully she started at one end of the window and checked each pair displayed. When she came to the end of the window, she whirled around and went into the store. A salesman came toward her.

"May I help you?"

She was breathless. "The pink slippers," she said, "the ones with high heels you had in the window two weeks ago—"

"Pretty," the salesman said, nodding.

"Are they gone?"

"What size do you wear?" he asked.

"I'm not sure."

Jane sat down and removed her shoe. The salesman sat on a low stool and whistled softly as he placed a ruler under her foot. "Stand up," he said.

Jane stood up. He nodded, checked the measurement, and strode jauntily to the stock room.

It was only then that Jane realized that she was sitting in a shoe store being fitted for the slippers her mother had said she couldn't have. Her mother wouldn't buy them for her, and she didn't have enough money to buy them herself. Jane took a long breath and held it for a second before exhaling slowly. She looked toward the stock room door. Maybe he wouldn't have the slippers in her size, she thought, half-hopefully; that would solve everything. On the other hand, if he didn't have them, she felt it would break her heart. She smiled ruefully and glanced toward the entrance. Charlotte and Judy stood on the other side of the door, pressing their faces against the glass.

Jane half-rose and beckoned, and the girls pushed the door open and came hurrying toward her.

"You're buying them!" Judy cried.

Charlotte said, "I knew your mother would see the light."

Jane frowned and shook her head. "I'm just trying them on," she whispered. "I couldn't resist trying them on. But I'm not going to buy them."

The salesman came toward them from the stock room, with a box held high above his head. He smiled all the way across the floor, and Jane's heart sank.

"Yes," he said, "we have them! This is the last pair, and it's your size." He put one of the slippers on her right foot. It looked rather odd over the white anklet she wearing, but the girls sighed ecstatically.

"Oh, Jane," said Judy. "They *are* just perfect!"

"They make your feet look as big as that." Charlotte measured an almost infinitesimal distance with both index fingers.

Jane twisted her foot this way and that, and she couldn't help smiling.

The salesman's hand hovered over her foot. "Shall I wrap them up for you?"

"Oh, no!" Jane said. "I mean, I'm not ready to buy them today. How much did you say they are?" she said hopefully. Perhaps, she thought, the slippers had been reduced.

The salesman picked up the box and read the figures on the end. "Only twelve dollars and ninety-five cents," he said. "A real bargain!"

Jane sat looking at her feet. If only she had more time, she thought. The salesman seemed to read her mind. "Shall I hold them for you?" he asked.

She looked at him. "Oh, would you? I mean, that would be just wonderful if you would. I'm sure I'll be able to get them soon."

The salesman took a pencil from behind his ear. He grinned at her. "I'll put 'hold until club dance' on it," he said.

Charlotte and Judy giggled, and Jane blushed. Then, with Judy on one side of her and Charlotte on the other, she walked across the deep carpet and out of the store.

"Wasn't he just darling?" said Charlotte.

"Oh, Charlotte!" Judy protested. "You think all men and boys are 'just darling.'"

Charlotte turned a bland face toward her. "Well, aren't they?"

Judy laughed and Jane joined in. They were both so nice, thought Jane suddenly, walking between them. She decided Charlotte and Judy were the nicest girls she had ever known.

CHAPTER NINE

The dance was four weeks away. Jane had never been so busy or so happy as she was during those four weeks. She took every baby-sitting job she could get. Sometimes it was only an hour here or an hour there, but she saved every penny she earned. She decided she wouldn't ask Merilee for the five cents she had borrowed; somehow she was reluctant to do that. But she didn't go to the Clearmeadow Stables to ride. Not once. She walked downtown instead of taking the bus. She bought no sodas, Cokes, or candy. The pink slippers, she was determined, would be hers.

The summer days flew by. The club dance was three weeks away, then two. Jane helped her mother iron curtains and shake out rugs. She cleaned desk and bureau drawers, washed windows, and repainted the window sill in the bathroom. She put on heavy gloves and helped her father trim the blackberry bushes behind the garage. She had hoped that Dad would offer to pay her for this job. When he didn't, she tried not to show her disappointment.

She spent an undeterminable amount of time on the

telephone talking with Merilee and Judy and Charlotte, discussing all the aspects of the glorious evening to come.

If she were downstairs, she used the telephone in the kitchen, being careful to close the door between the kitchen and the living room, or to speak low, almost in a whisper, if her mother were in the room. But Jane preferred to use the upstairs extension. If the phone rang when she was downstairs, she usually took the stairs two at a time and answered directly from the upstairs extension. For the importance of the calls was such that she could not discuss them with her mother. Charlotte, for instance, called to get her opinion on the matter of flowers.

If your date brings flowers, should you pin them on at home, or should you take them to the dance in the box? After many calls, Charlotte and Jane decided that it was perfectly all right to pin the flowers on at home; but if you preferred, it was also perfectly all right to take them to the club and pin them on there. Of course, you would have the problem of what to do with the box. And it might be a little difficult to excuse yourself from your date, the very first thing, and go to the powder room to pin on the flowers.

As the night of the club dance drew nearer, the telephone rang incessantly. It rang in the morning before Jane had finished her breakfast. It rang intermittently throughout the day. It rang in the evening after she had gone to bed. There was a tacit understanding in the family that, since the calls were inevitably for her, it was Jane who should answer.

She displayed her dress so often that her mother told her father she fully expected the gown to be worn out before the dance. Jane acknowledged the quip with the faintest of smiles. She hadn't expected her mother to understand how important it was for her friends to see and approve of her dress.

Privately she thought the white formal was just as pretty as any of the girls' dresses, even prettier than most of them. Merilee's new formal (she did get a new one) was cut rather low in the neck. Judy bought a lovely bouffant thing that was just right for her. Charlotte had a yellow organdy that was a bit tight unless she remembered to hold her stomach in. But, all in all, everyone was going to look beautiful.

Frederick would arrive tomorrow. The dance was only one week away, and Jane's happiness was complete.

That is, it would be complete this afternoon. For this afternoon she would take the money from her top drawer and buy the pink slippers.

She hadn't known how much she wanted the slippers until she had gone into the store and tried them on. She closed her eyes and saw herself wearing the dress and the pink slippers.

"Perfect! Just absolutely perfect!"

Jane smiled as she counted out the money. She had exactly twelve dollars and ninety-five cents. The salesman at Langleys' had been so nice to hold the slippers for her. But he wouldn't have to hold them any more. Because this afternoon she was going to buy them.

Jane hummed. She stuffed the nickles and dimes and quarters into her zipper bag and went downstairs. Her mother was bringing in the mail.

"I'm going downtown for an hour," Jane said. "I'll be back in plenty of time to help you polish the furniture."

Mrs. Taylor nodded. She riffled through the letters in her hand. Jane pulled out her lipstick and faced the hall mirror. She applied her lipstick lightly.

"Anything for me?" she asked. She was sure there wasn't. But it sounded so—well, so grown-up.

"Here's something for you." Her mother handed her a long envelope, and took her own mail into the kitchen.

Jane took the envelope and looked at it, amazed. There was her name, on the outside. She tore it open, and pulled out a thin typewritten sheet. Jane looked at the letterhead. It was a notice from the public library.

"You are hereby notified," it began. She read it through. It was a *bill,* a bill for three dollars and ninety-five cents! She was charged for a book that hadn't been returned. Jane sat down on the hall chair.

It's a mistake, she thought. She looked at the envelope again. Her name was on it. She re-read the letter. This was ridiculous! She had no book—

Suddenly the title of the book sprang at her from the letter. That was the book Merilee had returned for her weeks ago!

Quickly she went upstairs to the extension telephone. She dialed Merilee's number, and waited stubbornly when there was no answer.

At last, she heard Merilee's "Hello."

"Merilee," said Jane, "did you return that book of mine?"

"What book?"

"That library book of mine. Did you return it?" She didn't wait for a reply but went on, "Because I just got a bill for it from the library—for three dollars and ninety-five cents."

There was a short silence. Then Merilee said, "Of course, I returned it. Don't you remember? I gave it to you."

Jane swallowed. "When?"

"Oh, for goodness sake!" exclaimed Merilee. "Why should I want to keep your library book, anyway? Sure I returned it to you. I remember it distinctly!"

"When?" Jane repeated.

"Oh, ages ago. How do I know when?"

Jane said, and her voice was shaky, "Merilee, you know very well you never returned it."

Merilee laughed. "Oh, there you go getting *serious* again about a silly old book. Well, don't blame me if you can't take care of your books. Good-by. I've got to go now."

Jane listened to the click of the receiver; slowly she put down the telephone. Slowly she walked down the hall and into her bedroom. She opened her bulging zipper pouch and counted out three dollars and ninety-five cents in nickels and dimes and quarters. She wrapped the coins in the letter from the public library, and walked downstairs.

"Oh, I thought you had gone downtown," Mrs. Taylor said.

"No," said Jane. "I changed my mind."

She walked down the street to the library. She would never be able to make up that three dollars and ninety-five cents before the dance. The dance was next Saturday night.

Frederick was coming tomorrow. Tomorrow was Sunday.

But it wasn't losing the pink slippers that hurt the most. It was the way that Merilee had betrayed her. Betray was the word. Merilee, Jane could see now, had betrayed her many times during the course of their friendship. It was something she had never seen before. Jane walked faster. She might as well be truthful and admit that she had "pretended" not to see it.

Here was the library. Jane went in and pushed the package of coins across the loan desk.

The librarian read the letter. "Oh, isn't it a shame you have to pay for the book." She smiled at Jane. "If it turns up, bring it in, and we'll refund the amount—less the library fines, of course."

Jane nodded, turned, and marched out, still thinking of Merilee. She had been enchanted with Merilee, she thought, smiling wryly to herself. She knew that she was now disenchanted—completely.

In a way, it was her own fault. She should never have depended on Merilee who was so changeable. But it was Merilee's changeable disposition that had attracted Jane in the first place. She tried to be honest about it. Merilee's changes of mood had fascinated her. You never knew what Merilee would say or do or think of next.

She wondered if that was what her mother had meant when she'd said, "Merilee isn't a bit like you." Had her mother meant that to be friends people had to be exactly alike? Jane shook her head. No, if that were true nobody could ever have a friend. Then suddenly she realized what her mother had meant. To be good friends, people had to *understand* each other, or they had to have some basis for understanding. They had to believe that the same things were important.

Jane thought library books were important, and Merilee didn't. Merilee thought that politeness and punctuality were "bothers," and Jane thought they were obligations. Jane thought that telling the truth was necessary, and Merilee thought it made no difference.

Yes, she saw that she and Merilee had never really been "best friends" at all. She saw now that they never could be. They were too different. Jane could go on liking Merilee for her gayety and her love of fun. But Merilee could never hurt her again because Jane would no longer expect real friendship from her.

As she hurried home, she decided that she must telephone Judy at once. She must tell her that Frederick was expected to arrive tomorrow. If only she could have the pink slippers to wear to the club dance!

As she turned up the walk to her house, it occurred to her that she might ask her mother to lend her the three dollars and ninety-five cents so that she could buy the slippers. It would be an advance on her allowance. It wasn't very much to ask, Jane decided.

CHAPTER TEN

"And they'd be perfect with the dress," Jane concluded. "Just absolutely perfect."

Her mother was dusting the legs of the dining-room table; she shook her head. "Now, Jane," she said firmly, "your white flats are almost new and they're entirely suitable."

Suitable. Jane made a face. "But these would be perfect," she said again. "And I only need three dollars and ninety-five cents."

Mrs. Taylor refused to become excited. "I'm sure lots of the girls will be wearing flats," she said calmly.

"Charlotte's mother is buying her slippers with heels," Jane said pointedly.

Her mother shrugged. Out of patience, Jane turned to leave the room. She didn't exactly flounce—that would be childish—but she did show by the swing of her shoulders what she thought of her mother's lack of understanding.

"Jane!" The sharpness of her mother's tone made her halt. Jane turned reluctantly.

Mrs. Taylor spoke carefully. "You might take this dust cloth and finish the chairs. I must check on the oven."

Jane looked at the dust cloth her mother had placed in her hands.

"And do the sideboard, too."

Jane pressed her lips into a straight line. After all, her mother didn't have to tell her every single little thing. She could see that the sideboard hadn't been dusted, couldn't she? She began to dust a chair, her resentment growing. It wasn't fair for her mother to treat her like a child. She wondered if her mother realized that she was almost grown up. Jane tossed her head—and bumped it on a corner of the sideboard.

"Ouch!"

"Did you bump your head?" her mother called cheerfully from the kitchen.

Jane silently counted to twenty, rubbing her forehead. "Yes, I bumped my head," she responded coldly.

Her mother looked in from the kitchen. If she had heard the wrath in Jane's voice, she made no mention of it.

"When you finish," she said, "you may set the table. Your Uncle Gordon and Aunt Harriet and Frederick will be here for dinner tonight."

"Tonight!" Jane looked at her mother. "But I thought they were coming tomorrow!"

"They made better time than they expected to. Harriet phoned while you were out," Mrs. Taylor said. "Frederick will sleep on the studio couch in the den."

She walked slowly around the table. "We'll put Gordon and Harriet on this side, and you and Frederick can sit opposite them. That will give you a chance to get acquainted with him."

Jane looked at the table. It hadn't occurred to her that she would have to *talk* to Frederick. So far he had been only a vague, tall figure who would take her to the dance and guide her around the floor in time to the music.

Silently she finished the dusting. She set the table, then escaped to her room. Standing before her dressing-table mirror, Jane looked at herself. Then she turned quickly and went to the extension telephone. She dialed Judy's number. When Judy answered, she identified herself quickly.

"It's Jane," she said, and added hoarsely, "he's coming tonight!" She hung up quickly and made her way back to her room.

It was seven o'clock when they heard the car stop in front of the house. Mr. Taylor folded the newspaper he had been reading and laid it on the table beside him. Mrs. Taylor hurried to the door. Jane stood in the hall, behind her mother and father, with the welcoming smile she had practiced already on her face.

Over her mother's head she saw the car door open. Aunt Harriet emerged; her handbag was large and her hat was low over her eyes.

"Harriet looks very smart, as usual," Mrs. Taylor murmured.

Uncle Gordon stepped out of the car. Jane's parents

were hurrying across the porch. She heard her father whistle softly. "Same old Gordie," he said.

Jane followed her parents, watching eagerly to see the third passenger come from the car.

"Get a move on, Freddie," shouted Uncle Gordon, much more loudly than necessary, thought Jane, since he was standing beside the car.

And then from the rear seat came Frederick. He was short and thin; he looked about ten years old.

"Mother!" Jane gasped. It was a strangled sound.

But her mother didn't hear her. She was on the lawn, embracing Aunt Harriet and Uncle Gordon.

"And this is Freddie!" boomed Uncle Gordon.

"How do you do?" said Frederick. He wore braces on his teeth.

"Whoa there!" said Uncle Gordon with exaggerated astonishment. "Don't tell me— This can't be Jane?"

Jane felt ten feet tall. She smiled weakly.

"Well! How she's grown!" exclaimed Aunt Harriet.

Jane writhed inwardly under her aunt's scrutiny, but she turned her cheek for Aunt Harriet's cool kiss.

"You'd never know that these children are the same age," Aunt Harriet said.

Jane looked beseechingly at her mother. Mrs. Taylor frowned at her.

Somehow Jane got through dinner. When she was asked a question, she answered it as briefly as possible. She kept her eyes on her plate, lifting them only when she had to clear the table. Freddie ignored her. He talked to

Mr. Taylor. He wanted to know the population of the city and its chief industries. Aunt Harriet beamed every time he opened his mouth. And Uncle Gordon was perfectly sickening the way he kept urging more servings of this or that on his nephew.

"We have all sorts of things planned," Mrs. Taylor was saying to Aunt Harriet.

Jane looked up quickly, warningly, but she couldn't catch her mother's eye.

"Wasn't it lucky that we could be here for the children's party?" said Aunt Harriet. She gazed fondly at Freddie.

"Oh, yes. The young people have been looking forward to the junior dance at the club all summer," Mrs. Taylor told her sister-in-law.

Jane looked at her mother accusingly. Then one ray of hope came to her. Perhaps Freddie didn't dance.

"Freddie loves to dance," said Aunt Harriet.

"We're going to take you on a tour of the city one day," Jane's mother said quickly. "And we'll drive to Mount Rainier on another."

There were polite murmurs of pleasure.

"We're going to have a day downtown on Thursday," Mrs. Taylor went on, "while the men go fishing."

"Say, Gordie," asked Mr. Taylor, "did I tell you I caught a fifteen-pound salmon last year?"

"And on Friday, we're going to the beach for a picnic!" Mrs. Taylor announced. "We thought you'd enjoy that."

"Hear that, Freddie?" demanded Uncle Gordon. "We're going on a picnic!"

Jane had all she could do to keep her lip from curling.

The way her uncle and aunt fawned on this child. She kept her face expressionless. They weren't going to get any co-operation from *her!*

Her mother looked at her. "Jane loves to ride. Do you ride, Freddie? Perhaps you two could go horseback riding."

"Thank you," said Freddie.

Jane didn't say anything.

Her mother rose, saying, "Jane, will you help me clear the table?"

In the kitchen, her mother quickly closed the door into the dining room.

"Mother!"

"Sh! They'll hear every word you say."

"I don't care!" Jane said. But she said it in a whisper.

Mrs. Taylor turned and looked at her. Her face was stern. Her voice when she spoke was angry but controlled. "No matter how you feel," she said sternly, "Freddie is a guest in our house. I expect you to treat him as such. You will be polite to him. You will even be nice to him."

Jane opened her mouth to protest.

Her mother went resolutely on. "He is looking forward to the club dance. Aunt Harriet told me so. *We,*" she emphasized the word slightly, "will not hurt either Aunt Harriet or Freddie by refusing to go."

Jane had all she could do to keep her voice down. "But he acts like a baby!"

"Oh, I don't know," her mother said lightly, now that she had made her point. She began to stack the dishes in the sink. "I can't say that he acts much younger than you do."

Jane glanced at her quickly, and then at the dish towel in her hand. The dance wasn't until next Saturday night. In the meantime, she'd think of something. The telephone rang. Jane answered it.

"Jane? This is Judy. Is Freddie there?"

Jane glanced over her shoulder at her mother. She held the mouthpiece close to her lips. "Yes." Then she added quickly, "I can't talk now. I'm helping Mother with the dishes."

"I'll call you later," said Judy.

Jane went back to the sink and picked up her towel. She dried the dishes in silence for a few moments.

She didn't know when she became aware of the loathsome insect on the floor, but she sensed it a few seconds before she saw it. She stood staring at it while the hair at the back of her neck felt as if it were rising. The thing looked like an enormous spider. Its body was as long as a pencil and its legs were black and hairy. It made a convulsive leap toward her.

Jane shrieked. Too late, she saw the insect was not a real one.

Her mother turned, startled. There was laughter from the hall. The insect rolled backward and Freddie pounced on it.

"It's my mechanical spider," he said. "It scared you, didn't it?" He laughed so hard at the anger on Jane's face that her father and her uncle and aunt came into the kitchen.

Mr. Taylor laughed shortly. But Uncle Gordon thought it was the most hilarious trick he'd ever seen, and

Aunt Harriet acted as though Freddie were too cute for words.

"Oh boy, Uncle Gordon," Freddie crowed, "you should have seen her jump!"

Jane tossed her head. The color was coming back to her face. Too much color. "I hate practical jokers!"

She glared at Freddie and, with what dignity she could muster, walked out of the kitchen and took refuge in her room. This was her date for the club dance! She shuddered and threw herself across the bed. The telephone rang. Jane sat up on her bed.

"Jane!" her father called, "it's for you."

Jane drew her hand across her eyes. Then she went into the hall and lifted the receiver. She waited until she heard the click that told her the downstairs phone had been hung up.

"Hello?"

"This is Charlotte. I'm at Judy's! We're just dying to hear what he's like."

Jane took a deep breath. "Terrible!" she whispered, barely moving her lips.

"Oh, Jane!"

"Well, I'll tell you one thing," Jane muttered. "I'm not going to the dance with *him!*" She heard her mother's steps on the stairs. "I'll call you later."

She walked back to her room with her head high and her shoulders rigid. She pretended not to see her mother look meaningly at her when she passed her in the hall.

The telephone rang again. Jane answered it.

"On your call to San Francisco," the operator said, "your party does not answer. We will keep trying."

"Whose call?" said Jane.

"I'm sorry," intoned the operator. "Will you please have Frederick Wright call Operator 35?"

Jane scribbled the number on a piece of paper. With her nose in the air, she walked downstairs.

"It's for you," she said coldly to Freddie. "You're to call this number."

Freddie looked at the paper. "Your handwriting's terrible," he said.

"It's his aunt in San Francisco," said Aunt Harriet. "Freddie has been trying to reach her all day to say 'Happy Birthday.' "

She heard her mother murmur, "How thoughtful of Freddie!"

Jane went up to her room and shut the door. She set her mouth in a thin, determined line. She decided that she would not go on the tour of the city with the visitors, nor on the ride to Mount Rainier. She would not accompany her mother and Aunt Harriet on any shopping trip, and if she had anything to say about it, she would not go to the beach picnic.

CHAPTER ELEVEN

Jane had nothing to say about it. The week plodded by nightmarishly, just as her mother had planned it.

On the tour of the city, Freddie was at least sufficiently interested in the sights to ignore her completely. He was interested in everything, in bridges and buildings and monuments and statistics. Fortunately he directed all of his enthusiastic exclamations and questions to Mr. Taylor. When they went to Mount Rainier, he took a "sample" of every rock he could find. Freddie, it seemed, planned to be a geologist. And he wasn't on the track team; he was on his school's debating team!

Whenever her father stopped the car at various points of interest, so that all of his passengers could get out, Jane wandered ahead or lagged behind the others, and managed to stand apart from them. It worked—almost always. If there was a view, she looked at it. If there was a monument, she read the inscription. Once there was a fence across the road with a horse behind it. The longing for a horse of her own came back to her suddenly. She crossed the road, and the horse came to meet her at the fence. She patted its neck and whispered into its ear.

"Oh, you beautiful thing," she said aloud. "If only you were mine!"

When she turned, she saw that Freddie had followed her; he had been watching her and listening to what she said. Jane walked back to the car.

Thursday brought blessed relief because her father and Uncle Gordon took Freddie fishing with them. At the week's end, Jane congratulated herself. She had kept two steps behind everybody throughout the week and had managed not to have to exchange more than two words with Freddie.

But on Friday morning, with the trunk of the car filled with picnic hampers, they all drove to the beach.

"Don't try to lift that hamper, Helen!" Aunt Harriet boomed when Mrs. Taylor began to unpack the car trunk. "It's too heavy for you. Let the men do it!"

Aunt Harriet seemed to have a propensity for taking over. She had ordered everyone around all week. She should have been a traffic cop, Jane thought.

"Gordon!" called Aunt Harriet. "The picnic basket, Gordon!"

Jane looked around the parking area above the beach; fortunately there were very few cars here. Aunt Harriet's loud voice and bossy manner embarrassed her. She sat in the car with her head down, pretending to look for something in her beach bag.

Jane waited until the others had started down the path to the beach. Then she took her lipstick from the bag, hurriedly pulled off the top and made dabs on her upper lip; she worked the pink into her lips with her little finger, and blotted it carefully with a tissue. She scrambled out of the car and walked slowly to the beach.

The beach was already theirs. Aunt Harriet sat on a blanket under the beach umbrella, with a cushion at her back. Beside her was a sewing bag containing her needle-point work. Scattered on the sand were towels, extra shoes for Freddie, a beach ball, and bags of assorted things somebody might want. Uncle Gordon and Jane's father were already dealing their cards for a game of rummy, and Mrs. Taylor had put on a pair of old sandals she wore in the garden. Freddie was running up and down the edge of the beach, acting as though he were seven.

The grownups were talking loudly, just as if they were at home in the Taylors' living room. Jane looked up and down the beach. She hoped no other picnickers would pass this particular spot. She sat down on the edge of the blanket, hugging her knees; she closed her eyes.

"For heaven's sake, Jane!"

Jane opened her eyes. Aunt Harriet was peering at her suspiciously, the way Jane had seen her mother look at a questionable head of lettuce in the supermarket.

"You're surely not wearing lipstick at your age!" said Aunt Harriet.

Mrs. Taylor said quietly, "She's fifteen, you know."

Jane jumped up and ran down to the water. She threw a stone and watched it skip. A pebble hit her shoulder. She didn't have to turn to know that Freddie had thrown it. Keeping her face expressionless, she knelt and dug a hole in the sand. She didn't say anything when Freddie pushed the mound of sand back into the hole with his heel. She turned her back when he stumbled against the sand castle she had half-heartedly begun.

But when he dropped something wet and slimy, which could only be a jellyfish, on her neck, she jumped up with a shriek; tears came to her eyes.

Aunt Harriet smoothed the piece of needle-point on her lap. "Oh, pshaw!" she said. "Freddie didn't hurt you, Jane. Besides he didn't mean it. He was only playing. Weren't you, Freddie? A girl of your age," she went on, folding her hands over the needle-point and glancing sharply at Jane's long legs, "shouldn't be scrambling around with boys anyway. Moreover, you're too old to be such a crybaby."

"I was *not* scrambling around with Freddie and I'm not crying!"

"H'mm," said Uncle Gordon, looking at Jane.

Jane sat down on the sand. She lowered her head, trying to hide her flushed face. She wished they would stop looking at her.

"Hah!" said her father, engrossed in the card game. "There! I've got you!"

Uncle Gordon turned back to the game.

"Jane," asked her mother kindly, "would you like a sandwich?"

"It seems to me," said Aunt Harriet in her loud voice, "that Jane is extremely tall for her age." She had not taken her eyes off Jane. "How tall are you, Jane?"

Jane's throat was tight. She shrugged her shoulders, not answering.

Freddie grinned at her. "She's as tall as a skyscraper, I'd say."

Jane saw the smile that Aunt Harriet didn't bother to hide. She hunched her shoulders.

Freddie strolled past her. "Skyscraper," he said under his breath.

She turned her head. Freddie wandered down the beach, picked up the beach ball that her father had tossed to him, and threw it toward her. "Here, Skyscraper! Catch!"

She turned, but not quickly enough. The ball bounced off her head. She scrambled after it, picked it up and threw it, with all her might—in the other direction.

"Hey!" yelled Freddie. "What did you do that for!"

"Jane!" Mrs. Taylor said sternly.

Aunt Harriet didn't say anything. Her look held words enough.

Freddie ran after the ball. They watched him, silently. He raced down the beach, stumbled over a half-buried piece of driftwood, and fell on his face. Jane couldn't help it. She chortled.

Aunt Harriet said it aloud this time. "I think you ought to be ashamed of yourself," she said. "That's what I think!"

"Well, now, who would like a sandwich?" Mrs. Taylor asked brightly. "Jane, dear, would you like a tuna-fish sandwich?"

Jane didn't want a tuna-fish sandwich, She jumped up. "No!" she said thickly. She turned and ran swiftly up the beach.

CHAPTER TWELVE

To be Jane was more than Jane could endure. She scrambled around the rocky point which jutted into the water, and ran up the beach on the other side of it. Here the rocks were dry and sharp, covered with seaweed and barnacles. Jane stumbled against a large stone, and the broken shells with which the beach was strewn scratched her ankles. This stretch of the beach wasn't good for swimming. There were no picnickers here.

She made her way up some rickety ladder-like steps set into the side of a bluff. There was a deserted summer shack up there, Jane knew. She climbed rapidly. Some of the water-soaked wooden rungs had rotted. Maybe it would solve everything if she fell and broke a leg. They couldn't make her go to the dance tomorrow night if she had a broken leg, she thought grimly.

But she reached the top of the bluff without mishap, and stood looking at the panorama of sea and sand and sky. She leaned against the crude railing, then sprang back quickly with a little cry as it sagged under her weight.

Slowly she climbed down the wooden steps to the safety of the beach.

Back there, out of sight around the point, were Uncle Gordon and her father, playing their interminable game of rummy, and Aunt Harriet and her mother under the beach umbrella. And, of course, there was Freddie.

Jane wondered what it would be like never to go back —to walk on and on, stumbling over the rocks and stones, cutting her hands and legs on the shells. On and on. She could almost see herself fading out of sight over the horizon. She shaded her eyes with her hands and looked out over the water where little wavelets of heat shimmered in the air.

It was then that she saw him, the fair-haired boy in the little boat skimming toward the shore. The boat rammed up on the beach. It was a clumsy affair, its once-blue paint peeled and chipped. The waves made a slapping sound against its sides.

"Oh," she called, "are you going to beach it here?"

He was a tall boy in faded, old jeans. He looked at her briefly. "It's a free country," he said. Then he carried the rope, frayed to hairiness in places, up the beach and looped it around a log half-buried in the sand.

Jane followed him and sat on the stump of the log to watch him. Slowly he circled the beach, his eyes on the ground. Every once in a while he bent and picked up a charred piece of wood, wood left from beach fires, already half-burned. She changed her position on the log so that she could see him better.

Slowly he circled the beach, his eyes on the ground.

Suddenly he turned toward her. "Look, kid," he said roughly, "weren't you going somewhere?"

Jane bent and rubbed at the scratches on her ankles; she shook her head.

He put both hands in the pockets of his jeans and looked at her. "Well, what are you waiting around here for?"

Jane bit her lip. "Nothing."

The boy snorted. Jane jumped up. Her chin was trembling and her cheeks felt hot. "I was just going."

He shrugged and turned his back on her. "Suit yourself," he said.

He went on with his search for wood, looking at her occasionally. Whenever their eyes met, Jane quickly shifted her glance—to the sky, to the bluff behind the beach, to the boats on the water. But the boy didn't tell her to go, and once he even smiled at her.

He made frequent trips back and forth from the boat and the spot he had chosen on the beach. He dumped a rolled-up bundle which was a sleeping bag on the sand, and he brought a flashlight, a small hatchet, and several parcels from the boat.

Jane drew closer to him. She was interested. "Are you going to stay here all night?"

"Yep."

"Here on the beach?"

"Yep."

"Alone?"

He laughed, flattered. "Sure!" he said.

She was frankly envious. "I wish I could!"

"Huh! You." He glanced at her curiously. "I bet your

116

mother would have fits. Where did you come from, any-way? Do you live around here?"

She hesitated before replying. "Somewhere around here."

"Do your folks have one of those summer places up there?" He waved toward the point.

Jane didn't answer.

"Well, I never saw you around here before. I bet you don't live here at all. I bet you're just here for a picnic!"

Jane didn't know why, but she denied everything. "I am not. I hate picnics! I came by myself. I'm here all alone." It was true, she thought; she had left the others on the beach; perhaps she wouldn't go back. She shook the hair out of her eyes and looked up at him. She fluttered her lashes the way Merilee did. "I—I go everywhere alone."

"Yeah?" he said. He wasn't interested.

"Anyway, I'm here alone."

"All right, princess, you're here alone. Say," he said, "do you know anything about fires?"

She shook her head, but went to stand near him.

"Well, blow," he said. "Blow hard! I can't get this darned thing started."

He had made a mound of shavings. Industriously he set about to get them to glow.

"Look," Jane said, picking up a cedar shingle. "My father always fans a fire with something to get it started."

"I thought you said you go everywhere alone."

"Well, he comes with me sometimes."

"What's your name?"

She hesitated only a second. "Jane." She added quickly, "Spelled with a y."

He looked at her curiously and she bit her lip. He smiled at her; it was a nice smile that showed his white teeth and put little flecks of light in his eyes.

"How old are you, Jane-with-a-y?"

"Sixteen—maybe."

"And maybe not, huh? Okay." He stirred the fire. "You didn't by any chance bring a lunch, did you, princess?"

She shook her head. He plunged his hand into one of the paper bags. "Well, that's too bad. Because I did. And I'm hungry."

Jane watched him string some weiners on a long stick. She thought of the picnic lunch she had missed. Why hadn't she taken that tuna sandwich?

"I'm kind of hungry," she said. "I forgot my lunch."

"Is that so?" He turned the stick. The smell of the roasting weiners was tantalizing.

A gust of smoke blew against her face and she blinked rapidly, wiping away the moisture that rose to her eyes.

The boy sandwiched a weiner neatly in a bun and thrust it toward her. "Here," he said. "I was only kidding."

Jane ate it greedily, taking large bites and swallowing quickly. She grinned at him as he toasted four more weiners on the stick.

"I'm from Vancouver," he said at last. "I'm visiting my grandmother down here." He gave her an almost friendly smile.

She looked over the water. "From Vancouver? In that boat?"

"I didn't say I'd just come. My grandmother lives on the island. I've been here almost a week. Every day I take my lunch and row around the island. Sometimes I camp on the beach overnight."

"I'm here on a picnic," Jane said in a small voice.

He picked up a pebble and tossed it into the water. "I know," he told her. "Our house is just over the bluff from where you parked your car. We saw you come. My grandmother knows your mother."

He smiled wryly. "Fact is, she wanted me to go down and introduce myself, but—"

Jane nodded understandingly. "My name is really Jane," she said. "Jane Taylor, but there's no y in Jane."

"I'll call you Jane-with-a-y," he said with mock seriousness. "My name is Bob, with two oo's. Bob Henderson."

She laughed, and jumped up.

"Hey, don't go!" He jumped up, too.

She heard the shout then, from far down the beach. "I have to go back," Jane said, but she didn't move.

"Look!" Bob cried. He pointed toward the water.

A great gull swooped down to skim over the waves. They watched as he dove and emerged with a silvery fish hanging from his bill. The fish's tail flapped crazily in the air.

The ripples of heat over the water, the rapacious bird, the frantic fish, and the moistness of her palms made Jane feel strange. She breathed in the smell of seaweed and wood smoke. Suddenly her head ached. There was sand in her hair and the sun was hot on her shoulders.

"Jane! Jane, come back!" the faraway voice called.

She turned to Bob. "Thank you. For the lunch and everything," she said.

Then she ran. The wind pulled at her hair. The pebbles on the beach, the broken shells, the seaweed crusted with barnacles bit at her feet, but she didn't feel them.

"I'm coming," she shouted into the wind. "I'm coming!"

CHAPTER THIRTEEN

They were all there, all but Freddie. Jane ran up to them, thankful that she didn't see Freddie. Aunt Harriet came to meet her. Jane saw the anxious expression on her face even before Aunt Harriet spoke.

"Didn't he find you? Didn't Freddie find you?" cried Aunt Harriet; her voice rose hysterically.

"No, I haven't seen him," Jane said.

Uncle Gordon's cigar fell from his mouth, and he didn't even notice it. He seized her by the arm. "Look, Jane," he said roughly, "are you sure you didn't see the boy?"

Mystified, Jane shook her head.

"Now, let's not get excited," Mrs. Taylor said. "No doubt he's just hiding, to scare us."

Aunt Harriet turned on her wrathfully. "Freddie wouldn't do such a thing!" she said. "Oh, he's fun-loving and he likes to tease, but I know he wouldn't do such a thing to us."

Jane was silent. It seemed to her that Freddie would

do exactly that, for a big joke. But in the face of Aunt Harriet's deep concern and utter faith, she couldn't say so.

"He can't have walked up the beach so very far," she began, trying to be helpful. "The tide's coming in and you really can't walk very far—" She stopped. The same thought occurred to all of them. Steep, high cliffs flanked much of the beach. At high tide there was no shore line.

The normal pinkness of Uncle Gordon's face faded. Aunt Harriet whispered, "He's not used to swimming in the ocean, in such cold water."

"Look, Daddy," said Jane, feeling sorry for Aunt Harriet, "why don't you walk up the beach as far as you can go—this way? And Uncle Gordon can walk down the beach the other way? I'll climb up on the bluff and see if Freddie went up there to pick berries or something."

"Good idea," said her father. Uncle Gordon nodded and hurried off.

Jane climbed to the top of the bluff. No, Freddie had not come up here. She looked seaward. But because bushes and trees hid much of the shore line from her view, she reluctantly concluded that nothing would be gained by trying to spot Freddie from this height.

It was then that she thought of Bob Henderson. She scrambled down the path and cut across the rocks to his camp site. She waved to him, as to an old friend, and he came to meet her.

"It's Freddie, the boy who came with us. He's disappeared, and he doesn't know the beach," she explained hurriedly. "We can't find him. Everybody's worried and—"

Bob seemed to understand the situation. He spoke matter-of-factly. "Chances are that he's just hiding to scare you all."

Jane breathed a sigh of relief. "That's exactly what Mother and I think." Then she frowned. "But the others don't think so."

"How old is this boy?" Bob asked.

"About my age," Jane said with a shrug. "But very immature—a real baby."

Bob grinned. "Oh? Well, maybe he's not so different from you."

Jane looked at him quickly. She remembered that was what her mother had said.

"Well, anyway, he's a practical joker," she said with a scowl. "I hate practical jokes."

"And you think this is one of his jokes?"

They had paused to look up at the bluffs. Jane considered the question.

"No," she said at last, "I don't think Aunt Harriet and Uncle Gordon could be so far gone on someone who would be that mean. I think he *is* lost, and maybe scared."

Bob grinned. "What you mean is that you hope he's not really lost, just good and scared."

Jane smiled at him. "Yes, that's exactly what I mean."

Bob shaded his eyes and looked out over the water. "He wouldn't swim out beyond his depth or anything like that, would he?"

Jane shook her head. "He isn't used to swimming in the ocean. I don't think he'd try it. No, he's more likely to be digging around somewhere for rocks or Indian relics. He's a nut on that kind of thing."

Bob looked at her. "I guess I'm sort of a nut, too," he said. "I looked for agates all day yesterday."

Jane bit her lip and blushed. "I used to, too," she admitted, "last summer."

"When you were a mere child?" said Bob, but he was smiling.

"I didn't have much luck," Jane admitted. "I used to hunt for Indian relics, too. I used to climb up that cliff." She waved toward the point. "There are some old caves there—"

Bob raised his head.

"Do you think maybe—" Jane began.

He nodded. "I think maybe!" he said. "Come on. I know just where you mean."

They walked briskly up the beach.

"I was up there just the other day," said Bob. "Fact is, I tried to crawl into one of the caves."

"But it was too small!" said Jane.

"No, I was too big!"

Jane laughed shortly, but her eyes were already scanning the face of the cliff. They began to climb.

The cliff was part clay, part rock. The whole face of it was lined with ledges and openings. Picnickers had carved their initials on the rocks. Some of the caves had been dug by boys, Jane knew, but some of them were natural openings—crevices in the rock, big enough to crawl into, but often dwindling to nothing. Freddie was probably blissfully crawling on his hands and knees, exploring one of the deeper crevices at this moment. She felt a surge of anger.

"Fred-die!" she called.

They waited. There was no answer.

"Look," Bob said, "if he's really inside one of these caves, he'll never hear you."

Jane squatted on a ledge. She stuck her head into a fairly large opening in the rocks. "Fred-die!" she shouted, and quickly drew her head back. There were crawly things in there. She didn't care to stick her head very far inside.

There was still no answer. Jane and Bob made their way from cave to cave, peering inside, shouting, and listening. When they reached the point where the rocky cliff fell away, they retraced their steps silently.

"Maybe he's back on the beach now," said Bob.

Jane shook her head. She could see the beach from this point. She saw two figures—Aunt Harriet and her mother. Far down the beach, she could see her father trudging along, and in the opposite direction she could see Uncle Gordon.

"Freddie!" she shouted. She cupped her hands around her mouth. "Where are you, Freddie?"

"Here."

Startled, Jane turned and looked around her. "Did you hear something?" she asked Bob.

"Help!" It was a faint, distant cry.

Bob gripped her arm. "He *is* down in one of those caves!" He put his hands up to his mouth. "Freddie!" he shouted. "Keep calling! We hear you. Where are you?"

Jane ran from cave to cave, calling, listening.

Suddenly Bob said, "Jane! Here!"

She turned quickly and made her way to where he crouched at one of the first openings they had come upon.

Bob stood up. "Stick your head down there and see if you can see anything," he said.

Jane got down on her hands and knees. Gingerly she pushed her head and shoulders into the opening. "Freddie!" she shouted.

"I'm stuck!" said Freddie's voice from the cave.

Jane almost laughed with relief. She peered into the darkness. "But I can't see you!"

When Freddie answered his voice was hoarse. "That's because this darned rock rolled in front of me!"

"Well, can't you push it out of the way?" called Jane.

"Not from this side," said Freddie. "The darned thing's pinned my foot under it."

Jane pulled her head out of the cave. "His foot's caught under a rock," she told Bob.

"Move away," said Bob. "Maybe I can crawl in and lift it."

Jane moved aside, and Bob began to crawl on his hands and knees. He crawled a few lengths, then he stopped.

"What's the matter?" asked Jane.

Bob backed out. "I'm too darned big," he said. "And the cave gets smaller before it gets bigger. But he can't be very far inside. I can see a pile of rocks just a little farther on."

Jane took a deep breath. She tried not to think of spiders. "Move over," she said. "I'll try it."

She dropped to her hands and knees and crawled into

the opening. Something brushed against her face, and she swallowed a scream. She crawled on. Bob was right. The pile of rocks was just a few lengths ahead.

"Freddie?" she called as she inched forward.

"I'm okay," said Freddie. "I just can't move."

Jane lay on her stomach and began to scoop the sand away from the rock. She could hear Freddie's breathing. He was lying face-down. He must have twisted around as he fell, for his leg was held at what must be a painful angle. A small stone rolled down from somewhere and bounced on Jane's head. A shower of pebbles fell from above. She buried her face in her arms and held her breath. What if the whole ceiling should cave in!

Freddie's hoarse whisper came to her. "It's okay now," he breathed.

She raised her head. It came to her almost as a surprise that Freddie was frightened. Just as scared as she was. Perhaps more scared. Because he couldn't move, and she could. She ignored the tiny ants crawling over her legs and the pebbles that dropped on her head, and began to work frantically, tearing her fingernails on the rock.

"Ugh!" she heard Freddie say.

Jane almost smiled. The ants must be walking over Freddie, too. Well, she could understand his revulsion, and he had to lie still. At least she was doing something. She grunted as she tugged at the rock. It moved slightly. Freddie groaned.

"Are you all right, Freddie?" Jane whispered. She seemed to be running out of breath.

"Sure!" said Freddie. But she could see his face now and the cheerful reply belied his grimace of pain.

She put all her weight against the rock. It moved. "There!" she said. "But your leg is sort of stuck in a crack. Can you move it?"

Freddie twisted around and took hold of his tennis shoe. He pulled his foot out of the crack. He groaned sharply.

"Are you sure you're all right?" Jane asked again.

"You crawl out first," said Freddie. "Then I'll follow you."

Jane began to move backward. Freddie inched along behind her, dragging one foot.

"Good girl!" said Bob as Jane backed from the opening.

Freddie came out on his hands and knees. He tried to stand up. "Ouch!" he said as his leg crumpled under his weight.

"What's the matter?" asked Bob.

Freddie winced. "I can't stand on it. I guess I twisted my ankle or something."

Bob and Jane made a seat with their clasped arms and, with Freddie's arms around their necks, they made their way down the steep slope to the beach. Freddie was surprisingly heavy for such a skinny boy, Jane thought.

"Okay?" said Bob, as if he had read her thoughts.

She nodded, and said, a little breathlessly, "Okay."

Freddie winced when she stumbled against a rock. Bob's grip on her arms steadied her.

The family had caught sight of them from far down the beach and began to hurry toward them. Aunt Harriet was in the lead. Her gait was stumbling and awkward in her anxiety to reach them.

Why, she really loves Freddie, Jane thought with surprise. Her eyes caught Bob's behind Freddie's head.

"Well, at least we don't have to go out looking for *them*," he said; they grinned at each other.

But it was Uncle Gordon who reached them first, followed by Jane's father. The two men relieved them of their burden.

Jane rubbed her arms. Bob dropped back and walked beside her. "Say," he said, "you're pretty strong for a girl."

She blushed. She wished suddenly that she had been the one to be rescued, instead of Freddie.

The men put Freddie on a blanket and Uncle Gordon felt of his ankle.

"You think it's broken?" asked Aunt Harriet.

"No!" said Uncle Gordon. "A slight sprain. Maybe not even that."

Jane stood there, now that the excitement was over, not knowing what to say. At last she mumbled, "This is Bob Henderson, Mother. His grandmother lives out here. She knows you."

Mrs. Taylor smiled at Bob. "Of course, you're Mrs. Hanks's grandson. She told me you were coming to visit her this summer."

Freddie spoke up. "Gee, Jane, I guess I won't be able to take you to the club dance now."

Jane stared at him incredulously. Had he really thought that she would go to the dance with him? Freddie returned her stare innocently.

"It's sure too bad," he went on, wincing as he moved his leg, "after you got a new dress and all, and saved the date for me. I'm sorry, Jane."

Bob said to Freddie, "Maybe Jane will go with me."

Jane gulped. She was afraid to look at Bob.

"Well," Mrs. Taylor said, "I think that would be very nice. Don't you think that would be very nice, Jane?"

Bob grinned. "Well, *I* think it would be very nice," he said. "And I'll call for you at eight-thirty tomorrow night, if you'll tell me your address."

Jane sat between her father and mother in the front of the car on the way home. Freddie sat between Aunt Harriet and Uncle Gordon in the back; he talked incessantly. He told about the cave in the cliff and how Jane had crawled in after him. Jane looked at her hands; her broken fingernails would look terrible tomorrow night! But she smiled.

Uncle Gordon leaned forward and put his hand on Jane's shoulder. He had to clear his throat twice before he could speak. He patted her shoulder.

"Jane, my girl," he said solemnly, "I think your action deserves a reward."

"Oh, no!" said Jane.

"Oh, yes," said Uncle Gordon and Aunt Harriet simultaneously.

"Now what do you want?" demanded Uncle Gordon. "Name it. You just name it."

Jane was silent.

"She wants a horse," Freddie told his uncle.

Jane turned her head quickly to look at him. How on earth did Freddie know that? Then she remembered the day they had driven to the country, when she had crossed the road to talk to the horse. Freddie had followed her, she recalled; he must have heard what she said.

"A horse?" Uncle Gordon was saying. He looked fondly at Jane. "Well, if that's what this girl wants, that's what she's going to get. I personally will—"

"Oh, no," Jane said again. She looked at her mother; Mrs. Taylor was shaking her head. "I mean— Well, thank you very much, Uncle Gordon, but I don't really want a horse now." And as she made the polite protest, she knew that she didn't really want a horse.

"Well, for heaven's sake!" Aunt Harriet exclaimed. "There must be something that you want."

"That's right," said Uncle Gordon who seemed reluctant to abandon his generous gesture.

Jane glanced at her mother and smiled. "I want," she said—and by closing her eyes she could see them—"I want pink slippers with high heels to wear to the dance tomorrow night."

CHAPTER FOURTEEN

Jane walked slowly down the stairs, her feet a little un-
steady in the high-heeled slippers. She wore the white
formal, and in one hand she carried a silk evening bag of
the same pink as the rose at her waist. The evening bag
was Aunt Harriet's gift.

Bob Henderson was waiting for her in the hall, with a
square, white box in one hand. He looked at Jane and
blinked.

"Well!" said Jane's father and Uncle Gordon simultaneously, while Mrs. Taylor smiled.

Aunt Harriet said, rather grudgingly Jane thought,
"You look very nice, Jane."

Then a long, low whistle came from the living room
where Freddie was sitting on the sofa. Jane's cheeks were
warm. This was the first time a boy had ever whistled at
her; though it was only Freddie, she felt that a genuine
compliment had been paid to her.

Bob shoved the white box into her hands. "Here," he said, "this is for you."

"For me!" Jane took the box, set it on the hall table, and lifted the lid. She parted the green wrapping. A corsage! It had not occurred to her that Bob would bring flowers.

"It's a gardenia," said Bob.

"Oh, how lovely. Thank you." Jane held the flower uncertainly. This was an awkward problem. How could she wear the gardenia on her dress? The pink rose at her waist was enough. Her mother came to her rescue.

"Pin it on your evening bag, dear," she said.

Jane smiled as she fastened the gardenia to her bag. Then, raising her eyes, she looked into the mirror. In it she saw Freddie in the living room behind her; she saw him rise and take three steps without a trace of a limp. Then he limped toward the hall.

She caught her breath sharply. Freddie could have gone to the dance tonight! But he was pretending his ankle was still painful, so that Jane wouldn't have to go with him. Because she had made it so plain that she didn't want to go with him. She bit her lip, overwhelmed with shame. She was ashamed of her smallness, her meanness, her childishness thoughout the whole week.

Jane glanced at Bob. He, too, had seen what she saw in the mirror. Their eyes met briefly.

She turned slowly. "Freddie, why don't you come to the dance, too?"

Freddie's mouth fell open. He looked questioningly at Jane.

"Oh, you won't have to dance if you don't feel like it,"

she said quickly. "But you can meet all the kids and everything."

Freddie's eyes were shining. "You mean it?" he exclaimed.

"Of course I mean it," Jane said.

Bob said, "Sure! Come along!"

"Well, I think that's a splendid idea," Mrs. Taylor beamed.

Aunt Harriet took Jane's hand and patted it. "You look lovely, dear," she said. There was no reservation in her voice now.

Freddie limped hastily up the stairs to change his clothes.

The clubhouse was transformed. As Jane stepped into the ballroom with her two escorts, she gasped at the wonderland before her. Festoons of pink paper blossoms were everywhere. At either side of the orchestra's platform was a pink-frosted tree set in a white tub. Pink and white and silver balloons billowed about the ceiling, and everywhere was music and laughter and color.

"Wow!" cried Freddie.

The first girl Jane saw was Merilee. Merilee glanced at her, then at Freddie, and then, more fixedly, at Bob. Jane saw Merilee's mouth open in a gasp. Jane had to press her lips together so that they wouldn't curl.

Merilee stopped dancing and, pulling Woody along, came quickly up to her. "Oh, Jane!" she cried, pretending she didn't see either Bob or Freddie. "Isn't this a marvelous party?"

"Marvelous!" Jane agreed warmly. Then she said, "Merilee, I don't believe you've met Freddie Wright or Bob Henderson." She smiled at Woody. "Woody Neilson." The boys shook hands.

"Oh," said Merilee, looking up at Bob. "I don't think I've ever seen you around here before."

Freddie piped up, "Well, you haven't seen me around here, either."

Merilee turned to Freddie.

Bob took Jane's hand. "Let's dance," he said, and she found herself whirling away with him. She looked over her shoulder.

"But Freddie!" she exclaimed. She felt a surge of annoyance that Freddie should have been so quickly attracted by Merilee's glib charm. Then she shook her head. Well, why shouldn't he?

"Freddie can take care of himself," said Bob. "So relax."

Jane laughed. "Yes, sir," she said.

They danced. Jane's skirt billowed about her. She laughed with amazed delight; she was following Bob perfectly. "Why, you're a good dancer!" she told him.

Bob bent his head to look at her. "Of course," he said smugly. "What did you expect?"

"I didn't expect anything," Jane said honestly. Then she gave herself up to the fun of dancing.

She saw Judy and her partner. "Oh, Judy!" Jane called. The two couples rocked to the beat of the music.

"Judy, I want you to meet Bob Henderson," Jane said.

"Bob Henderson!" exclaimed Judy, then she added

quickly, "How do you do." She looked curiously at Jane before she introduced Barry to Bob.

The boys nodded to each other. Bob began to dance Jane away.

"Freddie's here, too," she called to Judy over Bob's shoulder.

When the music stopped, Jane and Bob made their way back to Freddie. He was sitting on a sofa, surrounded by a group of interested listeners that included high school juniors and seniors. Freddie was enjoying himself thoroughly.

"Well, whatever—" began Jane.

Bob said, "I thought he didn't know anyone."

"Well, he does now," she said dryly.

Then she heard what Freddie was saying: ". . . Only Jane could do it. She crawled in that cave and dug out the rock that had me pinned down. And that's how she saved my life!"

"Oh, my goodness!" said Jane, aghast.

Bob laughed. "Well, it's true, isn't it?"

"Not quite." Then she laughed, too. "Well, Freddie certainly knows how to take care of himself—outside a cave," she said.

"Let's get some punch," said Bob.

Jane breathed a sigh of relief. They sat on a window-seat and sipped the ice-cold punch. But they didn't sit there alone for more than five minutes. Freddie's story had spread swiftly around the room, and Jane was the center of interest.

During the next three numbers, Bob and Jane could

dance only a few steps together because of the boys who cut in. They all wanted to hear about Freddie's rescue from Jane, and she patiently went through the simple story five times before she was allowed to dance with Bob again.

"You know," she said, "I could almost tie Freddie up and toss him back in that cave."

"I'll help you," said Bob as he steered her away from another stag headed their way.

They traded dances with several couples—with Charlotte and her cousin, with Judy and Barry, and even with Merilee and Woody.

Jane looked at Woody curiously when he took her hand to lead her out to the floor. It was strange, but there was no queer little leap of her heart now.

Two months ago, she would have swooned with joy—as Merilee would say—if Woody had asked her to dance. She remembered how nervous she had been at Judy's party. It had never occurred to her then to enjoy herself. She had been too busy thinking about her shortcomings and about what others thought of her. She had been filled with anxiety all that evening. No wonder she hadn't even been able to smile naturally. She smiled now.

"You know," said Woody, "you're different."

"Well, I'm certainly different from Merilee," Jane answered, because that was what she had been thinking. Then she went on quickly, "I mean, Merilee is so gay and talkative. I'm more quiet, naturally."

Woody looked at her admiringly. "Action speaks louder than words sometimes," he said.

137

He was referring to Freddie's rescue, of course, and Jane made a little face. But she couldn't help feeling pleased.

Woody twirled her in a more intricate step. Suddenly he said, "You know, I half expected you to give me the old freeze again tonight."

Jane looked at him, amazed. "Me? Freeze?"

"B'rr!" said Woody, pretending to shiver. "Every time you looked at me your face was stiffer than a board."

Jane giggled, remembering the egg facial. Woody was fun, when you got to know him. But Bob was nicer, and even Freddie had turned out to be a pretty good sort, too.

The music stopped with a crash of the cymbals, and supper was announced.

"What are you grinning at?" Bob asked, as he handed her a paper plate that held a scoop of potato salad and a ham sandwich.

"At my thoughts," Jane said promptly.

"You mean you *think*, too?" He made it sound like a compliment.

"I was thinking that boys can be fun," she said, biting into her sandwich.

Bob sat down beside her, balancing his plate on his knee. "I think I'd better keep my eyes on you," he said.

". . . when you get to know them," Jane added, helping herself to the pickle on his plate.

But the old feeling of awkwardness came over her when it was time to say good night to Bob. Jane had never said good night to a boy after a date. Of course, Freddie made it easier, for they helped him into the house from Bob's car, all three of them still pretending that his limp was genuine. But now Freddie had disappeared.

Jane stood with Bob at the door. "Thank you very much. I had a wonderful time," she said, more formally than she had intended to.

"It was good of you to let me take you," Bob said politely.

She looked up at him. "Oh, no, it was good of you to—"

Suddenly they were both laughing. Then they said good night, and Bob drove away. Jane heard a door opening and closing, and she followed the sound into kitchen. Freddie was examining the contents of the refrigerator.

"For heaven's sake," she said, "you're not hungry after all that punch and food, are you?"

"I'm always hungry." Freddie waved a chicken leg at her. "Want one?"

"Sure," Jane laughed.

They sat companionably at the kitchen table, munching chicken legs and drinking milk. Jane's thoughts were still on the club dance.

"A wonderful, wonderful party," she sighed happily.

Freddie nodded. Well, he had certainly seemed to enjoy himself; he'd had a group around him all evening. Then she remembered that Freddie hadn't danced. "Freddie loves to dance," Aunt Harriet had said.

Jane leaned across the table. "How's your ankle, Freddie?" she asked.

He grinned. "Something the matter with my ankle?"

Jane set her glass of milk on the table and gazed at him. "You really were faking, weren't you?"

He shook his head. "Not at first. It really did hurt, at first."

She was silent for a moment, before saying, "It's been a crazy week, hasn't it?"

"Crazy," Freddie agreed.

Jane looked at her hands; the pink polish had successfully camouflaged her broken fingernails. "I guess I haven't been very nice," she said regretfully. "I'm sorry."

Freddie shrugged. "I don't blame you. I guess I was no bargain, either."

"That horrible spider!" she shuddered.

Freddie had the grace to look ashamed. "Say, I'm really sorry about that. It was a gadget Uncle Gordon found in a joke store in San Francisco. He couldn't wait for me to try it on someone. He thought it was such a great trick that I felt I owed it to him to try it on someone. But I'm sorry it was you."

"Oh, that's all right," said Jane. "Do you want some more chicken?"

"No, I'd better get to bed. Uncle Gordon said he wants to start for home early in the morning."

"I'm sorry you have to leave tomorrow," Jane told him.

As she carried the glasses and plates to the sink to be rinsed and stacked, she reflected how easy it was to be mistaken about people, how misleading first impressions could be. Freddie had turned out to be so nice, and she had missed a lot of fun all week by being mean and resentful.

They walked into the hall. At the stairway, Jane turned to him. "Good night, Freddie," she said.

"How's your ankle, Freddie?" she asked.

He looked at her earnestly. "Jane," he said, "will you write to me?"

She couldn't resist it. "My handwriting's terrible," she reminded him. They both laughed.

"But I will," she promised. "I really will write to you, Freddie."

Jane went quietly up the stairs. The pink slippers hurt her feet, and she took them off when she reached the landing. She saw that a light was still burning in her parents' room.

Jane peeked in. They were both asleep. A magazine lay on Mrs. Taylor's bed, and Jane knew that her mother had intended to stay awake, to ask about the party.

She tiptoed into the room, picked up the magazine, and placed it on the chest of drawers. Then she bent and kissed her mother's cheek. Mrs. Taylor's eyes flew open.

"I had a perfectly wonderful time!" Jane said softly.

Her mother's eyes closed, and a contented smile drifted over her face. Jane turned off the bed lamp.

Her father sat up suddenly in his bed. "Who's that?" he demanded in a sleepy but startled voice.

Jane stifled a giggle. "Go to sleep," she whispered. "It's only Jane."

B